LISTEN

LISTEN

SOURLAND MOUNTAIN SERIES BOOK 2

KRISTIN MCGLOTHLIN

This is a work of fiction. Names, characters, organizations, places, events, and incidents are either products of the author's imagination or are used fictitiously.

Published by Bird Upstairs, Seattle
www.birdupstairs.com

Produced by Girl Friday Productions
www.girlfridayproductions.com

Design: Paul Barrett
Development & editorial: Alexander Rigby
Production Editorial: Laura Dailey
Cover illustration: Kristina Swarner

ISBN (hardcover): 978-1-7363579-1-0
ISBN (paperback): 978-1-7363243-3-2
ISBN (ebook): 978-1-7363243-4-9

Library of Congress Control Number: 2021903861

First edition
Printed in the United States of America

This book is dedicated to the jazz artists
Susannah McCorkle (1946–2001)
and Roy Hargrove (1969–2018).

Heaven is so lucky to hear them play!

There was a child went forth every day,
And the first object he looked upon and
received with wonder or pity or love or
dread, that object he became,
And that object became part of him for the day
or a certain part of the day . . .

—*Leaves of Grass* by Walt Whitman

Sourland Mountain is in central New Jersey, twenty minutes from the town of Princeton. On top of the mountain sit two neighborhoods. The first neighborhood has similar style homes with well-kept lawns and paved streets. They have plenty of land around them and are buffered by woods. North of it is the Backwoods of Sourland Mountain. The houses there are eclectic and not all of the roads are paved. The homes in this neighborhood back up to the park and wildlife sanctuary named the Sourland Mountain Preserve.

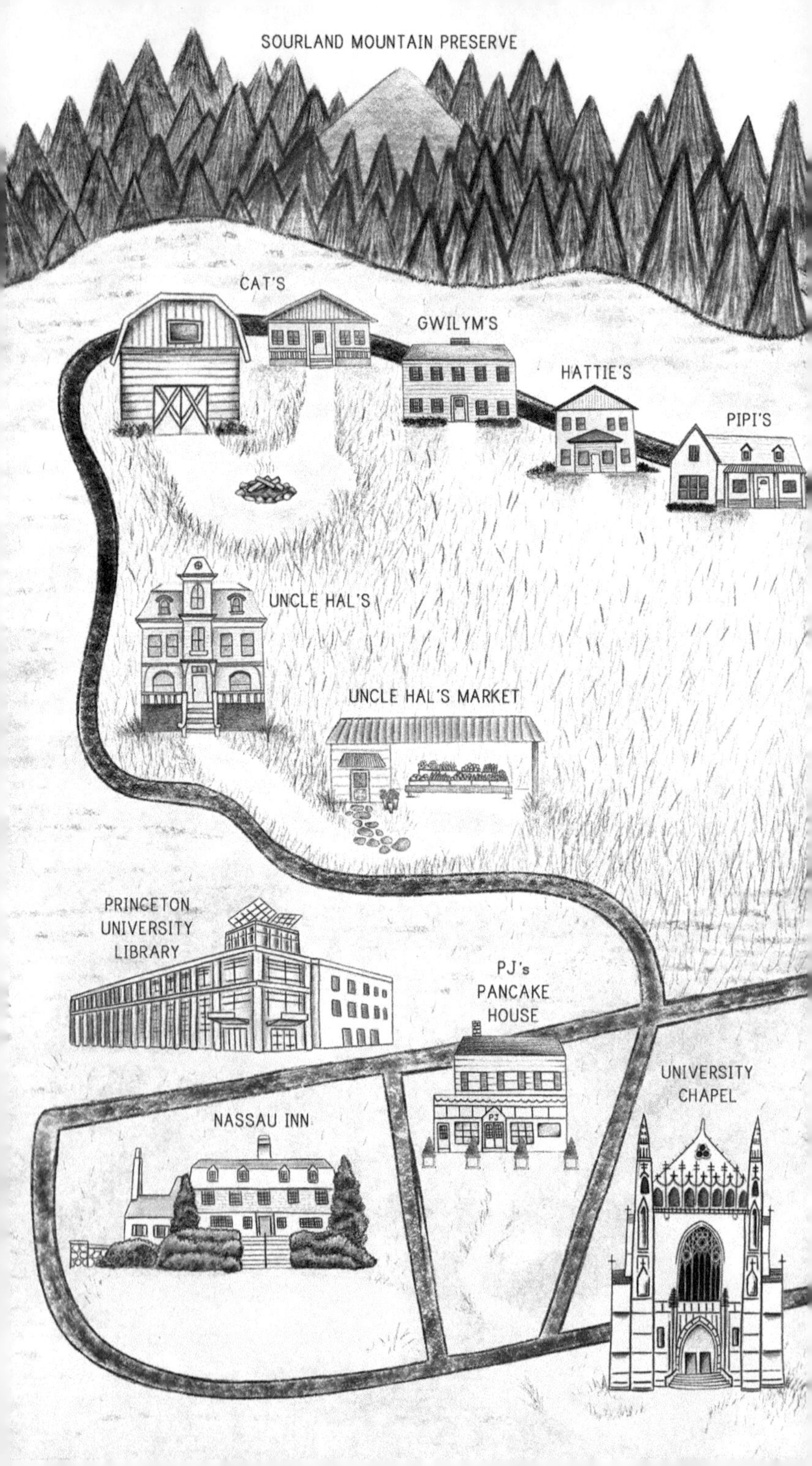
SOURLAND MOUNTAIN PRESERVE
CAT'S
GWILYM'S
HATTIE'S
PIPI'S
UNCLE HAL'S
UNCLE HAL'S MARKET
PRINCETON UNIVERSITY LIBRARY
PJ's PANCAKE HOUSE
PJ
UNIVERSITY CHAPEL
NASSAU INN

JOE'S
LIBRARY
LIBRARY
GEORGE'S
RIVER'S
OLD BARN
PARTY
TOOLS
MOVIE
MUSIC
TIGER'S TALE
ART

NOVEMBER

Gwilym Duckworthy traipsed past the row of birch trees that marked the property line between his yard and his friend Cat Hamilton's family field. The Hamiltons' annual Thanksgiving football game had just ended. His team had lost. Gwilym swept the reddish-blond hair from his freckled forehead, then stuffed his hands in his jeans pockets. He shivered in the chilly autumn air. His red team had included Cat's uncle Hal and Benton Whitman, the artist who rented the Hamiltons' studio-barn; the winning blue team had been his cousin Hattie Crucible, Cat's dad, and Cat's brother, Buddy. Gwilym and Hattie had played in the game every year since they'd been old enough to catch and throw a football.

This year had been different. A car accident with her mom in August had left Cat in a wheelchair. Her legs had taken the impact of their car hitting a tree, leaving her with casts on her legs. Because she couldn't play, Cat designated herself as the referee, taking over the position usually held by her dad or Uncle Hal. She was the first female referee in the history of the Hamiltons' Thanksgiving football game. Hattie was selected by Buddy to play quarterback. Cat had hemmed and hawed to Gwilym that she wasn't happy Hattie was going to be the first-ever girl quarterback in the game. But he had told Cat (and found out later her mom had told her, too) that Hattie was just warming up the position for her to take over next year. Gwilym was glad it had been Buddy's decision, because he wouldn't want to have to pick between his best friend and his cousin.

Gwilym looked forward to the game every year, glad to be included in Cat's family tradition. Unlike other holidays, at least on Thanksgiving he could enjoy someone else's family and, for a few hours, not think about the family member who had been absent from his life since he was three years old: his mom, who had left Gwilym, his brother, Clay, his sister, Bex, and his dad ten years ago to pursue a career as the leader of a jazz band.

Even the scent of burning leaves, his favorite smell this time of year, couldn't stop Gwilym from grumbling to himself about Cat's unfair penalty call that had led to his team's defeat. He took the game seriously, as did everyone else. The competition became fierce when the players took the field. He didn't want to admit that he'd been responsible for his team's loss.

He heard leaves crunching behind him.

"And the MVP award goes to Hattie Crucible, the first girl quarterback of the Hamilton Thanksgiving football game! And the crowd goes crazy! Haaaaa!"

Gwilym saw the exuberant expression on his cousin's face. Still, he couldn't help repeating his complaint about Cat's penalty call. "I'm just saying that—" He stopped, seeing Hattie's pout. "Yes, Hattie, you were an excellent quarterback today."

"Thank you," she said, looking appeased. Then she shivered. The wind picked up her ponytail and whipped it against her shoulder. "I hope we don't have to take many pictures of things outside for the scavenger hunt. It's cold out here."

His phone signaled an incoming text. "Clay says they'll meet us at the front door."

When they reached the house, Hattie said, "Hey, I just thought of something. Cat and her family include us every year in their Thanksgiving game. Why haven't we invited them to play our family scavenger hunt?"

"Maybe we should," he said. He didn't feel that way inside. The scavenger hunt was a tradition they began after their mom had left them. Although Gwilym missed her terribly, the hunt was something she couldn't take away from him.

"I bet Bex would play if Buddy did," she said, nudging Gwilym's shoulder. The image of his sister's pretty face came into his mind. He didn't know if Bex had dated any boys yet.

"Maybe," Gwilym answered. As he and his cousin approached the front door, the faces of Gwilym's family members came into his mind: Hattie was Chinese, Bex was Black, and Clay had been born with Down syndrome. He rarely thought of the diversity in his family, but it always made him happy that they were all different.

Clay stepped out the front door and smiled. His sky-blue eyes shone through his glasses and his blond hair glowed in the sun that had popped out from the clouds. Gwilym glanced at his brother's short, stocky figure. He was impressed with Clay's dedication to the scavenger hunt, especially because it meant the football teams missed out on a mean competitor. Clay chose the items for the scavenger hunt list. Their stepmom, Ferguson, had given him the responsibility. The first few years of the hunt, he had made handwritten lists of things to find, which he'd given out with a bag to put them in. Now he texted the list and they took photos of each object with their phones.

"Hi, Gwilym. Hi, Hattie," Clay said. Before Clay closed the front door, Gwilym heard the adults inside laughing, which warmed his heart. "Did you get the list I texted you?"

Bex slid out the door and stood beside Clay. Bex loved to bake. And like Clay, she was dedicated to contributing to her family's Thanksgiving traditions, and therefore didn't play in the football game. Gwilym noticed flour on Bex's face just as Clay reached out to wipe it off.

"What are you doing?" she asked, jerking away from Clay's hand.

"You have flour on your forehead," he said, softly brushing away the powder. Watching his brother doing this stirred a memory of Clay making the same motion, only wiping tears from Bex's cheeks. A wave of heat swept across Gwilym's chest.

"Can we start?" asked Hattie. "I'm freezing." Everyone nodded and looked at their phones.

Gwilym read the list.

CLAY'S SCAVENGER HUNT LIST

- ☐ 1. acorn
- ☐ 2. squirrel
- ☐ 3. feather
- ☐ 4. favorite color
- ☐ 5. favorite object
- ☐ 6. favorite sound
- ☐ 7. favorite musician or band

"Same rules?" Hattie asked Clay.

Clay nodded. "The winner is the one who takes the seven photographs and gets to the kitchen counter first. Then I give a ribbon to the person who takes the best photo of each object."

Hattie scanned the list. "We have things to find outside like always. We've got a theme this year? Favorite things."

Clay beamed. "I wanted to take photographs of my favorite things."

"All right. I'm starting inside," Bex said, then added, smiling devilishly, "I don't know why you're all even bothering to play. I'm going to crush this game."

"Good luck!" Clay said.

"Good luck, everyone," Hattie repeated, with a little less sincerity than her cousin. "I'm getting the outside objects done, then warming up inside."

Gwilym nodded and headed to the backyard with her. His heartbeat sped up. He loved playing this game with her and his siblings. Walking toward his wooded backyard, Gwilym felt happy to have grown up on Sourland Mountain. There were three main areas: his neighborhood, with paved streets and manicured lawns and neat houses on large properties; the Backwoods, with dirt roads and mainly unkept homes and lawns. Some of these houses had lakefront views of Lake Saturday, where his grandpa had fished. Next to the lake was the Sourland Mountain Preserve, where he and his family rode their bikes.

"Acorn, feather, squirrel," Hattie sang. "Oh, acorns!"

Gwilym placed a mound of multicolored fall leaves on the ground, arranged some acorns on top, and took his first photo of the hunt.

"There's a squirrel in that tree!" shouted Hattie. Gwilym watched the furry creature with its flicking tail balance on a branch. "I think it'd be easier to video it," he said. So they recorded the animal as it bounced from limb to limb.

Then Gwilym separated from his cousin to search for a feather. A bird squawked in the tree beside the driveway, stopping him. "Hey, do you think you can leave a feather for me?" He walked around the tree. *Wouldn't you know it!* "Thank you!" He flung the feather into the air and, as it floated down, he took his shot.

He put a checkmark in the boxes on his phone.

☑ 1. acorn
☑ 2. squirrel
☑ 3. feather

- ☐ 4. favorite color
- ☐ 5. favorite object
- ☐ 6. favorite sound
- ☐ 7. favorite musician or band

My favorite color's green. What's green around here? He scanned the yard. *The hose!* He rushed around the side of the house to the gardening hose. He had a good idea, but he'd have to move quickly. He dragged it out from between some shrubs and the stairs that led to the laundry room door, then began bending it into a letter. He took a photograph of the shape. He then made another, and another, until he'd spelled the word C-O-W. Three photographs making one word. Gwilym chose cow because it wasn't too hard to make the letters and because there were still herds that lived on the two remaining farms on Sourland Mountain. He looked at his photos and nodded. *That didn't take too much time. Now a favorite thing.* His favorite thing was his red bike. He darted to the shed.

He blinked at the bright ceiling light inside the shed. Then he beamed with pride at the left-hand corner, the space where he'd made his own music studio. The only thing missing was the trumpet he'd rented. Gwilym had selected the trumpet to play in the school band, and his parents had okayed him to use the shed as his practice spot. Bex had told him she would drive him to Farrington's Music store in Rocky Hill to pick up the trumpet. He chose it because it was the instrument his mom played in her jazz band, the Caroline McCorkle Band. Gwilym had never played a musical instrument and was excited to see if he'd gotten any talent from his mom. He'd been told she was a gifted artist. He wanted to be as good as she was—or better!

A green tackle box he'd noticed while setting up his studio sat on the floor behind his bike, next to a stack of moving boxes. It had belonged to his grandpa, who died last year, and Gwilym intended to see what fishing gear and lures might still be inside. But that would have to come later. Right now, he needed a photo of his favorite thing. He took a shot of the bike, turned off the light, and closed the shed door.

Outside, the family's two Rottweilers, cinnamon-colored Baby and cocoa-colored Bear, ran up to him. Gwilym rubbed their heads as they sniffed and panted. *I'll record that for my favorite sound.*

The phone's microphone was interrupted by an incoming call. "No Caller ID" the screen read. A moment later it signaled a voice mail message. He ignored it. *I can't stop to see who it is right now.* Instead, he checked his list. One more object remained: favorite musician or band.

- [x] 1. acorn
- [x] 2. squirrel
- [x] 3. feather
- [x] 4. favorite color
- [x] 5. favorite object
- [x] 6. favorite sound
- [ ] 7. favorite musician or band

Gwilym didn't have a favorite musician or band. *Maybe when I start learning the trumpet I'll find a kind of music I like.* He went inside the house, immediately hearing a commotion in the kitchen. Gwilym realized he couldn't win without photographing all the objects.

"I won!" Clay shouted, drumming the marble counter with his hands.

Bex sat on the stool beside him. "Ha! Actually, Clay's lying. I was here first." Clay shook his head. "No you weren't."

Bex smiled mischievously at her brother.

Hattie glided past Gwilym. "Looks like you're last, Cuz!"

Clay announced the scavenger hunt officially over.

The adults were laughing at the ruckus. The parent-folk included Hattie's parents (Gwilym's Aunt Martie and Uncle George), Gwilym and Hattie's grandma, and Gwilym's dad and step-mom, Ferguson. Ferguson's squat body shook as she applauded, and her tiny, dark-brown eyes twinkled at Gwilym. If he could have seen his insides, he was sure they would be glowing. He was thankful she was part of his family. His dad and Ferguson had married four years after his mom had left them. That first year of their marriage, Gwilym, Bex, Clay, and Hattie had started the Thanksgiving scavenger hunt.

"Time for a smoke." Gwilym's grandma stood up, holding her lighter and cigarettes. She was a large woman, the opposite of Cat's slim, fit grandma. Gwilym's grandma's idea of exercising was getting up from the kitchen table and walking outside to sit on the patio chair. It didn't matter to him what physical shape she was in, Gwilym liked being with his grandma. She'd always been there for him and his siblings. The smell of cigarettes didn't bother him, though it did the rest of the family. When he joined her on the back porch, he liked concentrating on the swirling smoke making its way up to the sky. He'd go out with her after the Thanksgiving feast.

Gwilym and the other scavenger hunters headed for the family room for Clay's award ceremony. The last to leave the kitchen, Gwilym heard Ferguson's voice. "Do you remember how the scavenger hunt began, Harry? The kids started playing the year we were married. Clay was maybe fourteen, Bex would have been about twelve, and Gwilym must have been seven." She lowered her voice, but Gwilym could still hear her talking to the others. "Harry was taking a psychology course, the last credits needed to complete his associate's degree. He came home after class one night with the idea of a scavenger hunt. The professor had lectured on the subject of parental abandonment; how children who'd been abandoned by a parent often have an object they associate with the parent who left them. The professor called them 'background objects.'"

Gwilym's mind raced as he joined the scavenger hunters. *"Background objects." Do I have any?* If he did or didn't, the idea made sense. But he didn't want to think about something like that today.

The family room was darker than the kitchen, the light coming from two table lamps on either side of the leather couch and the glow from the TV screen. Clay sat between Bex and Hattie. Gwilym squatted beside the coffee table, where seven handmade ribbons were spread out, and an extra one in case of a tie.

"I like the rainbow-colored ribbons, Clay," Hattie said.

Clay grinned and sat up straight on the edge of the couch. "First," he said, putting up a finger, "is the photo of the acorn."

They passed around their phones. Hattie's photo was of multiple acorns on a tree stump.

"She's arranged them in a smiley face. Why hasn't anyone done that before?" Bex commented.

"I give Hattie the first ribbon," said Clay. Hattie raised her arms in victory.

Clay enjoyed watching both Hattie's and Gwilym's squirrel videos. "Squirrels are funny to watch, almost as much fun as cat videos." He awarded his brother the ribbon, saying the squirrel was the cutest in his video.

Hattie rolled her eyes. "Brothers sticking together."

Clay went on with his list. "Next is the photo of a feather."

The group agreed Gwilym should get the ribbon.

"Number four is favorite color," said Clay.

Smiling, Bex held up her phone. "My favorite color is orange." The case was orange with the Baltimore Orioles logo on the back in black. The Baltimore Orioles had been her favorite baseball team since she was a little girl. The Orioles had been their grandpa's team too. Bex would watch the games on TV with him while their grandma made them orange Jell-O. Softball became Bex's sport. And their grandpa was over the moon when she received a scholarship to play for Florida State University.

Clay informed her that her phone case was not a photograph. Bex argued the color was on the phone that takes the photos, so technically it was a part of the phone and therefore was a combination of favorite color and object.

Gwilym raised his eyebrows. "That's original."

"That's clever," said Hattie. She was usually very willing to agree with Bex. Gwilym knew she wanted to be just like her cousin.

Clay wasn't done with his sister's color choice. "Orange isn't your favorite color. Purple is your favorite color, like the color of your baby album."

Bex grabbed a pillow and clutched it. "Whatever. Can we move on?"

"What color did you pick, Hattie?" Gwilym asked.

"Turquoise," Hattie said. *"So . . ."* She glanced at Bex, who was staring at the floor. "I took a picture of the plastic turquoise mermaid stirrer Bex keeps on her dresser."

Bex looked at her. "You did?" Hattie blushed.

"I made the letters C-O-W with the garden hose since green's my favorite color," Gwilym said.

"Wow, Gwilym," said Hattie. "You're outdoing yourself this year. Clay?"

"My favorite color is blue," said Clay, "because I'm a boy. I took a picture of the blue cover of my baby book."

"Blue doesn't have to be for a boy," Bex said teasingly. Clay shrugged and looked down at the ribbons, then handed her one. "Best photo of a favorite color," he said.

"Yes!" she said.

"Number five is favorite object," Clay said. "My favorite object is my John Denver poster."

Gwilym showed the photo of his bike. Leaning over to view the picture, Clay exclaimed, "There's Grandpa's tackle box! You haven't gone fishing with us. You were too young when we went with Grandpa."

"I'd like to go sometime," agreed Gwilym. Then he asked Hattie what she'd chosen for her favorite object.

Hattie passed her phone around. "The rug Grandma hand-wove for me. I took a photo of Gwilym's rug because, of course, I'm not at home."

Gwilym enlarged the image of his rug. "Wow. You can really see the stain on the horse's head where I spilled soda, and the brown mane has blended into the red background in the spot where Baby threw up."

"And why," Bex asked, "is this your favorite object?" She released her grip on the pillow and carefully put it beside her.

"Because Grandma made one for each of us, which was sweet and must have taken a lot of work. And it's an heirloom, like Cat's great-great-grandma's mural on the wall of her family's barn."

"Good answer," Bex said, nodding.

"My favorite object," Bex said, pressing the face of the phone against her chest, "is . . ." She flipped the phone around to reveal her well-worn Metallica *Ride the Lightning* T-shirt.

"I thought the mermaid stirrer would be your favorite thing," said Clay. "When we were kids we saw Mom perform with her jazz band at a club in downtown Princeton. It was the only time we saw her play with her band. The stirrer came in Bex's Shirley Temple drink. She thought it was the most beautiful thing she'd ever seen. She carried it around like a stuffed animal. Now she keeps it in a ceramic bowl on her dresser." Gwilym and Hattie both commented that they hadn't heard that story.

"Maybe it's not my favorite thing now, Clay," Bex said.

Clay handed her a ribbon for the T-shirt picture. She knocked her shoulder against his and kissed his cheek, which he rubbed at, embarrassed.

The room was quiet for a moment until Gwilym said, "Sound is next."

Two sounds tied: Gwilym's recording of Baby's and Bear's huffing, and Hattie's of the electric mixer of "someone making the mashed potatoes."

"The last thing on this year's scavenger hunt list is favorite musician or band," said Clay.

"That's easy, Clay," Bex said. "You took a photo of your John Denver records."

"I did." Clay's cheeks reddened. "And you picked one of your Metallica albums. Hattie?"

"I couldn't think of where I could find a picture of my favorite music in your house. Then I remembered! There's a poster of *West Side Story* in the laundry room."

"That's Ferguson's poster. It's her favorite movie," said Clay.

"I love musicals," Hattie exclaimed. "I haven't gone to one yet. But someday I will."

The group turned to Gwilym. “I don’t have a favorite musician or band right now.”

“No?” asked Hattie.

“Maybe when I start playing the trumpet I’ll find a musician I like.”

Clay slowly placed the last ribbon on his own lap. Then he announced, “For the first time in the history of the Duckworthy/Crucible Thanksgiving Scavenger Hunt, we have a tie, with Hattie and Gwilym each receiving a ribbon for their sound. But the person who finished first and is the winner of the scavenger hunt is . . . Bex!” They cheered. “Okay, okay! Enough!” Bex said, her cheeks flushed.

“And next year, Clay,” said Hattie, “you should give yourself more than one ribbon.”

Gwilym switched from the floor to a chair beside the couch. His phone slipped out of his pocket when he moved. *Oh, I forgot to check the message.* He slipped it back into his pocket. *Probably no one important.* But then his mind snuck in the possibility that it could be his mom who’d called and left him a message . . . since it was a holiday? Would she want to check in? See how he was doing? *Would she? She wouldn’t have my number.* He glanced at Bex and Clay. *Had she ever called them?*

Gwilym decided to immerse himself in the football game instead of worrying whether his mom had called him. The earlier NFL game had been the Washington Redskins playing the Dallas Cowboys. Dallas beat Washington 31–23. The game about to start was the Detroit Lions against the Chicago Bears.

Tomorrow the routine he'd begun at the start of last school year would begin again, with breakfast at PJ's Pancake House in downtown Princeton.

FRIDAY

Gwilym woke up with a grin. This morning he was going to ride his bike to his favorite breakfast place, PJ's Pancake House on Nassau Street in Princeton. The place had the best coffee and biggest breakfast around. His waitress was usually Janine, who served him when he sat at the counter.

Rubbing his hands, still cold from the bike ride, Gwilym sat down at his regular seat. "The usual?" asked Janine as she filled the coffee cup in front of him. (He'd tasted coffee for the first time last year and liked it.) He nodded. Looking at the walls of the restaurant, he thought they must be coated with the smell of brewing coffee and maple syrup by now.

He laid his phone beside him, then picked it up and, without hesitating a moment longer, listened to the message from the previous day. "Hi, Gwilym," said a female voice that sounded vaguely familiar. "It's your mom." His heart jumped into a fast beat. "I hope you're doing well. I'm sure you are. The band and I will be in town this week. We're playing two nights at Princeton University and I'd like you, Bex, and Clay to come see us. So, I was wondering if we could meet, you and me. Maybe at a restaurant like—what was the name of your favorite restaurant in Skillman? Tiger's T-A-L-E or is it *T-A-I-L*? I remember you asked us if Tigger lived at Tiger's Tale. It was the only restaurant we could get you to eat at." She chuckled. A stream of heat ran across his chest. *Tiger's Tale.* He inhaled deeply. His cheek was sweaty against the phone. "We could meet for lunch or dinner if you'd like. Or someplace else. A place you like to eat at now. Let me know." He looked at the screen: forty-five seconds. He dropped the phone on the counter. Ten years and she'd finally called and left him a forty-five-second message. He swept his bangs from his forehead and looked around. The inside of the restaurant *felt* different to him now, but nothing *looked* different. The customers were still chatting; the cooks in the kitchen were still clanking the dishes. Janine came with his dish and her friendly smile. He stared at the pancakes on his plate, hoping he could get them down without throwing them up.

The pancakes stayed in his stomach. He walked to the bike rack, where he stopped, confused. "Where's my bike?" He looked up and down the street. *Where is it?* He couldn't understand. *I did ride it here, right? Of course I did. Did I forget to lock it up?* He'd have to call Bex and ask her to pick him up.

It didn't take her long to get there. When he got in the car she asked him, "Did you tell the people in the restaurant that your bike's gone?"

He clicked his seat belt. "Yes. They said I could post a flyer on the community message board."

"And you remember locking it like you usually do?"

"No." Tears welled in his eyes. *First Mom, now my bike? Great.*

"Dad bought you a good lock," Bex said. "I didn't think anybody could cut that cable."

"Yeah." He stared out the window at the drizzly weather. "I guess I forgot."

"I had to tell him and Ferguson why I was picking you up."

"I figured you'd have to." He sighed. He couldn't lose his bike. How would he get to PJ's? And he needed a bike for his job!

❧

"It was careless of you, Gwilym," his dad told him when he was back home in the kitchen. His dad and Ferguson were sitting with him at the table.

His stepmom suggested someone cut the lock. "You are usually very responsible, Gwilym. I can't imagine you'd forget to lock your bike," she said.

"Are you going to be careful with your trumpet?" his dad asked.

"Yes, I will. I promise."

"Because if you can't be, then maybe you shouldn't be allowed to play in the band," his dad continued.

Gwilym felt nauseated again like he had in PJ's, and put his hand on his stomach where he imagined the pancakes were now flipping.

His dad's tone softened. "We'll make signs to post round Princeton. Hopefully someone will return it or find it and call us or the restaurant."

"How am I going to deliver the baskets for Uncle Hal?"

"Maybe Clay will let you borrow his bike," Ferguson offered. Her suggestion made Gwilym relax a bit. He didn't want to lose his job because he didn't have a way to deliver Uncle Hal's produce orders. And now he really needed to make money to buy himself another bike if his wasn't returned.

SATURDAY

Uncle Hal was Cat's mom's brother. He lived in the original farmhouse on the family land that used to be a working farm. Next to the house he had planted a large garden of fruits and vegetables, which he sold at his market stand that he and Cat's dad and brother had built at the edge of the property. Uncle Hal's veg and fruit stand had become a local success story. Gwilym delivered Uncle Hal's produce in baskets to clients on Sourland Mountain.

Clay's bike, slightly larger than Gwilym's, was awkward for Gwilym to ride down Sourland Mountain. In the distance, customers gathered around Uncle Hal's stand, everyone bundled in jackets and coats. As he came closer, he hit the brakes. Underneath the sign that read "Hal's Vegetable & Fruit Market," a tall woman with shoulder-length reddish-blonde hair stood, selecting some root vegetables. He got off the bike and moved behind a tree. Uncle Hal seemed to recognize her. Gwilym watched Hal walk over and hug her. When she turned in Gwilym's direction, he instantly recognized her face. It was his mom, Caroline Duckworthy, or Caroline McCorkle now. He placed his hand on his nose as he stared at hers, and looked at the color of her hair. They were the same. He leaned on the tree for support. *I can't go there now. I'm not ready to see her. I'm not ready for her to see me.*

He waited, gripping the tree trunk. *They know each other.* Gwilym hadn't realized his mom and Uncle Hal knew each other. He glanced around the tree to see his mom get in a car and drive off in the direction of Princeton, away from where he was hiding. Gwilym hopped back on the bike and pedaled fast to the stand.

"Hey, Gwilym," said Uncle Hal.

"I'm sorry I'm late," he said, his heart beating so fast he imagined it bursting from his chest. He quickly attached a basket for delivery to the back of the bike. "I'll be back."

He felt the intense strain on his leg muscles as he pedaled up the mountain. With each time his foot pushed down the pedal, another question rolled through his head. *Had she visited Aunt Martie? Hattie would be home. Could she have met his mom?* So many questions.

When Gwilym returned, a car was driving off, leaving Uncle Hal by himself. He urged Gwilym, "Hey, slow down. No rush to get these baskets out. Relax a minute." He leaned back against the table and crossed his arms over his solid chest. Gwilym did the same.

They watched the scenery together. A bird flew by; the wind blew the corners of the tablecloths. "Beautiful day." Uncle Hal ruffled his hair. "Seems to be better than the last, though not as beautiful as the next."

Gwilym agreed. "Despite the cold," he added, and started to relax. He'd been uncertain if Uncle Hal would tell him his mom had just been at the market stand. But it seemed unlikely, since that wouldn't be a casual conversation topic: *"Oh, by the way, your mom stopped by . . ."*

"That's not your bike, is it?"

"No. It's Clay's bike. Mine's gone missing."

"Oh, sorry." Uncle Hal looked at his feet, then out to the road. In a whisper he added, "It'll be okay." Then in his normal voice he said, "Gwilym—hey, Cat told me you're going to play the trumpet! That's great! I used to play—Yes, sir?" A customer had come over to them. "What are you looking for? Right over here, sir." Uncle Hal guided the man toward what he wanted to purchase.

"I'll get on the next delivery," Gwilym called to Uncle Hal, who waved to him.

He grabbed the next basket and checked the name tag: "Crucible." Hattie's house. *Of course, I can ask Aunt Martie if she gave Mom my phone number.*

Riding back up the hill to his neighborhood, Gwilym thought about when he should return his mom's call. He could *not* call her back, but that was something Bex would do, not him. He decided he definitely wouldn't call her today. Gwilym had seen his mom for the first time in ten years, since he was three years old—that was enough for him to take in right now. And maybe she didn't really expect him—or want him—to call her back right away. *Maybe she just called to make herself feel better.* She'd made the effort to contact at least one of her kids. *Why did it have to be me? Or was she going to call Bex and Clay too?*

He parked the bike at Aunt Martie's garage door and went in. His aunt was sitting at the kitchen island typing on her laptop, with papers and folders spread across the counter. "Hi, Gwilym." She pushed her bifocals up on her nose. "Brought me my order?"

"Yes. Uncle Hal put in some extra winter squash he thought you'd like." After setting the basket on the corner of the counter by his aunt's work, he took a step back, put his hands in his back pockets, and rocked on his heels.

"Hal's such a sweet man. Thank you, Gwilym." He didn't move. She took off her glasses and looked at him. "Is there something else?"

He'd just have to ask. "Did you give my mom my phone number?"

"Yes," she said.

His eyes widened. He hadn't expected her to answer so honestly. "Why?"

"Because she asked me to." She closed her laptop. "I wondered if you'd ask me."

"I don't understand why you'd do that. Did you give her Bex's or Clay's?"

"She wanted to get in touch with you." She crossed her arms and leaned back.

"I didn't even know you had my number," he said.

"Sure, I have all the family's numbers. All the parent-folk do in case of an emergency."

"Oh." Gwilym didn't speak for a moment. Then he thought of something. "Why didn't you ask me first if she could have it?"

"You're right, Gwilym." She paused. "Considering your feelings would have been the right thing to do, the thoughtful thing. I'm sorry."

"Did she say why she wanted to talk to me?" He sat on the stool next to her at the counter.

"She didn't say."

"And you gave my number to her anyway?" That familiar wave of heat raced across his chest.

"Gwilym," she said in a parental voice. "I decided to give her your number because I believe she wants to see you and Bex and Clay. She's ready to see you again. Do you think you can give her another chance?"

"Again? Like the first time counted for me?" His hands closed into fists.

"It's been difficult for her *too,* Gwilym, to be away from you three all these years. But she stayed in touch with me."

His legs felt like cement. "For ten years you've talked to her?"

Aunt Martie was now standing next to him. "She stayed in contact with me. She's kept up with what's happened in your lives."

"Has she been in touch with anyone else in the family?"

"No. At least, not to my knowledge."

"I'm supposed to feel better knowing she took time to call you?" As he waited for her response, he heard music playing softly upstairs. *Hattie must be in her room.* He hoped she wasn't listening.

"Your mom tried to make it work, being both a mom and a professional musician. But by the time her band became successful, she had you three."

"Didn't she want us?"

"Yes, of course she did. Let me see if I can explain. Your mom wanted to be a musician ever since we were children. She played in our middle school and high school bands, then got into Princeton University's music program. Your mom is also very confident, which sometimes drives her to do what she wants no matter what the consequences may be. But Gwilym, she's a good person. She made the decision to leave your family because she felt she'd make everyone miserable if she stayed."

"Couldn't she have stayed with the family and still traveled with her band?"

She nodded. "I suppose she could have. But they were offered a yearlong tour in Europe, and that made it very hard to be a mom and a wife and to have the career that she wanted."

His heart sank. *A career she wanted more than she wanted us.*

Before he could say his thought out loud, she tried to reassure him. "They did try, your parents, to keep the family together while she was gone. But in the band's beginning, they didn't make much money. Definitely not enough to allow her to travel back and forth from Europe to the United States."

"Why didn't we all go with her—be together *and* Mom could have her band?"

"That might have worked. But your dad . . . he really didn't want to go. His life was here. I think he felt his wife should be here too."

"But that doesn't seem fair to Mom."

"No, it wasn't."

He sighed heavily, then asked what he'd always wondered. "Why did they have three children if they knew she wanted to travel the world in a jazz band?" His heart pounded, anticipating her answer.

"Your mom and dad wanted children. They loved each other very much, Gwilym, even after they separated, then divorced." She shook her head. "It's hard to explain grown-ups."

"It shouldn't be that hard," said Gwilym, annoyed with this common thing grown-ups said.

"They had Clay and they were so happy. Then your parents adopted Bex because they wanted to give a home to a child who needed one. As you know, your uncle and I couldn't have a baby, so we decided to adopt too after seeing what a wonderful experience it was for your parents and Clay. We went through the long process to adopt, then traveled to China and brought Hattie home with us."

Gwilym wasn't convinced that it was all so happy back then. "Bex was eight when Mom left, and Clay was ten. I was three—so when did she decide to form a jazz band and leave us? Why did she have me?"

When his aunt looked at him, he could tell she was thinking about how she could explain to him this complicated situation. *Tell me Mom didn't want me. Tell me it's my fault she left.*

"You were a surprise."

Oh. Gwilym hadn't heard this before.

"They weren't planning on a third child—but they were filled with joy when they found out they were pregnant. I know that sounds like a parent thing to say. It's true, though. Really, Gwilym. Your mom loves you, just like your dad and Ferguson do."

His head was cloudy and his whole body felt like cement had been poured into it.

"I don't know what else to say to you. I'm not saying what your mom did was right. I'm not saying she made the right decision leaving you." She paused, staring at the kitchen countertop. "After she left, you all had plenty of adults to take care of you: your grandma and grandpa, me and your uncle George, and of course your dad, and then Ferguson."

"But you don't think she made the right decision?" he asked.

"It's not what I would have done. She really hurt you and Bex and Clay, and of course, your dad. It was good when he married Ferguson. And you know, you and Bex and Clay were always cared for. We all took care of you three and your dad before he met your stepmom. We did the best we could. You three were loved by all the family who cared for you."

Gwilym was embarrassed that so many people had needed to step into the job of raising him and his siblings—the job their mom was supposed to be a part of, that had been her responsibility. "Thanks, Aunt Martie." He stood up and put his hand on her shoulder. "Thanks for talking to me and being honest about how you feel." They exchanged weak but loving smiles. "I guess I should go now."

Once outside, he felt exhausted. What should he do? He was supposed to go back to Uncle Hal's market and pick up the next order. But his head was so stuffed with emotions that he didn't think he could ride his bike—Clay's bike—straight. He walked it down the hill, concentrating on the market coming more into focus even as tears burned his eyes. But he didn't want Uncle Hal to see that something was wrong. When Gwilym got to the stand, he realized he didn't have to worry, because Uncle Hal was busy loading up another basket.

❧

That night Gwilym went into his music studio. Inside the shed was one ceiling light. During the day, the overhead bulb and the two windows gave the room enough light for him to read by, but at night there wasn't enough to illuminate his area. Luckily, he'd found a standing lamp while moving boxes. It was shining light on two boxes next to the music stand and a wooden stool. Gwilym leaned over to read their contents. On the top box, "Baby clothes & albums" was written in marker; on the bottom one he read the scribbled words, "Records & Record player." He put the top box on the concrete floor, then sat down and opened the one containing the music. The records were stacked upright next to the record player. Carefully, he pulled out the records and placed them so they lay flat on the floor. He set the record player beside them. When he plugged it in, the turntable began rotating. Gwilym, fascinated with the buttons on this machine he'd never seen before, located the Off button, then placed the first record on the player and moved the needle onto it with the utmost delicacy. The first record he played was John Coltrane's *Blue Train.*

Looking closely at the album cover, he gasped and nearly dropped it. His middle name was Coltrane. *Coltrane. How cool is that!* He had never known the significance of his middle name. His mom must have chosen it. *I'm named after John Coltrane! I'm named after John Coltrane!* He envisioned telling his music teacher. "No way!" she'd say. "That is so cool!" Everyone in the school band would be blown away! Gwilym wished he could find a photograph of his mom playing in her band to show his teacher and the kids at school, but he knew there wasn't one in the baby books.

Gwilym examined again the front of the album cover. It had a black background with "John Coltrane" in green, like the color of the garden hose, then below was "BLUE TRAIN" and "blue note 95326" in white. These words and numbers, and their meanings, were insignificant next to the photograph of the artist, which cast him in a cool blue light. Looking like he was in his thirties, Coltrane's left arm was bent with his hand behind his head, and his right hand was resting against his bottom lip. He was contemplating something. Something serious—like how he was going to play the next tune? Or was he just thinking he was hungry and wanted a sandwich? Whichever it was (probably the former), it didn't matter, because this was the portrait of a master. Gwilym stared at the puckered creases in Coltrane's brow. *Wow.* He got how important jazz music was from the musician's expression. How seriously he'd have to take learning and practicing if he wanted to be a good jazz trumpeter. Even more so now that he knew he'd been named after this jazz legend.

The speakers below the turntable were small, but the sound was clear. Gwilym got a chill, not from the tune, but from the cool night air. He got up and switched on the space heater, then sat back down and leaned against the wood wall. He closed his eyes and began bobbing his head to the beat of the first tune. The music went fast, then slow, then up and down; at moments it sounded like it was screaming, then whispering. The music was like a ball bouncing from corner to corner, side to side. He swung his arms and swayed his body in time with it. He was surprised by how much he liked it right away. *This is cool! This is it. I'm playing jazz when I get my trumpet.* His heart pumped furiously. He was swept away by the music.

He carefully picked up the needle, then placed it on the next record, by the jazz musician George Benson. Gwilym grinned at the bright colors on the cover and Benson's smile. Benson's music was upbeat and the tunes sounded more like what he'd heard on the radio. This was like the soft jazz that Cat's dad listened to in the car. He enjoyed listening to this style of jazz, but the music didn't bring out emotions in him like Coltrane's music.

With his arms wrapped around his legs, Gwilym swayed and tapped his feet to the new beats and rhythms. He listened to the first tunes on albums by Miles Davis, Charlie Parker, Cassandra Wilson, Cab Calloway, Ella Fitzgerald, Billie Holiday, and Dianne Reeves. Picking up the needle after a piece by Roy Hargrove ended, Gwilym let out a *Whoa!* His brain and body were exhilarated. One last album lay on the floor, titled *The Majesty of the Blues,* by Wynton Marsalis. Gwilym would listen to it next time. He recognized the musician's name, and the image on the album cover looked familiar too. The picture consisted of a simple cutout of a black figure with a small red dot on its chest and surrounded by six yellow stars, all on a blue background. Maybe he'd pulled a book on this artist from the library shelf when he and Hattie and Cat had collected art books for a report they each had done in October.

These were most likely his mom's albums. A pang of jealousy went through him as he imagined young Clay and Bex listening to these albums with her. The only memory Gwilym had of his mom was from his crib. She had come in to pick him up when he was crying. He'd nestled his face into the crook of her shoulder, into her warm bathrobe, which he remembered was covered in yellow daisies.

Gwilym shook away the memory and pulled over the box with the baby clothes and albums. Clay's album was on top, "Clay Ford Duckworthy" printed on the blue cover. The first photo was of Clay as a newborn, wrapped in a blanket and held by their mom. Another picture was of him with their dad and mom and both sets of grandparents. The album was completely filled with handwritten captions under the photos, probably added by their mom. He set Clay's album aside and pulled out the next one. "Beth Caroline Duckworthy" was printed on the purple cover. Bex had been given their mom's name as her middle name. In the first photo, Bex was propped up on their mom's lap. Her eyes were closed and her mouth was a little pink circle. "One week old" was written below the photograph of the day they brought Bex home. He flipped through pages of his adopted sister smiling like he never remembered. She looked like a happy baby in those photographs.

His red album was labeled "Gwilym Coltrane Duckworthy." His cheeks became warm as he turned each page, gripping the laminated edges. Anxiety began filling him up. He knew what was coming. Halfway through the album his mom started disappearing from the photos. Eventually, she was completely gone, replaced by Aunt Martie and Uncle George, his grandma and grandpa, and his dad, Clay, Bex, and Hattie. Even Cat made appearances in some photos. He closed the book and looked in the bottom of the box.

An assortment of cards and letters and pieces of paper were jumbled together. On top were two concert ticket stubs for Nnenna Freelon and her jazz band. He pulled out Christmas- and birthday-present tags; cards from gifts of flowers, all of them signed "Love, Harry"; and a torn piece from a Reese's Peanut Butter Cup wrapper. He turned the scrap of paper over. "To Caroline, My Good Friend. Lots o' Luck, Harry."

He found birthday, Christmas, Halloween, St. Patrick's Day, and Valentine's Day cards. He read a few, then stopped. He got the gist of them. The interesting thing was how his dad's handwriting had changed on the cards. One Halloween card explained, "I'm trying a new writing style. I'm going to use it from now on. Do you like it?"

Gwilym stretched his legs out as he examined the pile. Why were they here and not with her or at his grandma's house? There didn't seem to be a box or folder they had been in. His dad would have organized everything, kept each card in its envelope, and the loose items would have been placed inside another envelope and labeled. Gwilym smiled, thinking about his dad's fussiness. He was always telling them, "You have to be ready for anything to happen to you. You must be organized." Gwilym took out the remaining papers. They were typed letters with an address that looked like the address for Buddy's dorm room at Florida State

University, which Gwilym had seen on an envelope on Cat's kitchen counter.

He opened the first letter.

> *August 4th*
>
> *Caroline,*
>
> *Once again, I find myself wondering why I'm here and not in music school somewhere. I guess it means it's about midsemester: happens every time. But I've kept in a good mood, thanks to some brilliant weather that won't quit. Every day seems to be better than the last, though not as beautiful as the next (kind of like my hairstyle) . . .*
>
> *Yours, H*

Gwilym read the beginning of the letter again. He laughed and set the piece of paper on top of the pile. He gazed into the shed past his pool of light to where he could just make out the neatly stacked boxes. *So many family memories in here. What other important family artifacts were in these boxes?* Their house had a crawl space, no basement, and that was why they had the shed. Gwilym had played in here with Hattie and Cat when they were little. Their toys were probably in one of the boxes.

He was excited about the chance to read something that his dad had written back in college. Find out some things he didn't know about his dad—like since when was his dad so funny! And since when did he want to go to music school? He didn't remember his dad or anyone in his family mentioning that. In fact, his dad never offered much information about when he was young. *Maybe I'm being too nosy. Maybe I shouldn't read them? Bex would read them!*

Gwilym decided he would read all the letters even if it was being nosy. Maybe he could learn more about his mom, since his family had barely told him about her. He glanced around the shed and spotted his grandpa's green metal tackle box. He knelt down and opened it. Inside he found a shiny fluorescent green, yellow, and orange lure, and there was just enough room to hold the letters. Before shutting the shed door, he went back and got it. He would keep the tackle box containing the letters in his bedroom.

SUNDAY

Gwilym had been in Farrington's Music store in Rocky Hill, the small town near Princeton, many times. When he had walked past the different instruments the store sold and rented, he wanted to try each one. He had been most interested in what the store owner, Joe, told him were brass and woodwind instruments. Joe willingly handed Gwilym a trombone, saxophone, clarinet, even a tuba to try out. But when Gwilym blew into the trumpet for the first time, he knew this was his instrument. He loved the sound of it, the feel of pressing down on the valves, and the look of the shiny brass. He was aware that it was what his mom played, so it wasn't a mystery to him that he was drawn to the trumpet. *I have her hair color; why couldn't I have music in my bones like her, too?*

Gwilym called the store on Sunday morning, and Joe confirmed that Gwilym's trumpet was ready for him to pick up.

Bex was all set to take him to the store. While she was driving, they played their college logo game, which she had devised for them to play together in the car. It was simple: they each tried to be first to call out the name of the college for the logo sticker on the back of a car. Bex and Gwilym really started watching college football together after Grandpa died. Gwilym thought it must be important to her to watch a sport with someone in the family, and he was glad he was the one.

"Georgia!" his sister shouted and nodded to the bumper sticker on the car in front of them. "GW," she added, pointing to another car in front of them, this one with a sticker on the back window.

"George Washington," Gwilym answered.

When they pulled up to a stop sign, Bex squinted at another car in front of them, this one with a *G* in the window. "This one is tricky," she said. "My first guess would be Georgia. But the *G* doesn't look like the Georgia logo."

"There's no red, either," said Gwilym. "It's black and white." The car stayed in front of them. "It could be Green Bay."

"Or Grambling. If it wasn't in black and white . . ." The car with the *G* sticker turned left. Bex smacked the steering wheel with her hand. "Hoyas."

"Hoyas? How'd you get Hoyas from a *G*?"

"Because I have that T-shirt Dad got me—from Georgetown. Georgetown Hoyas!"

"Wouldn't their logo be an *H*?"

"An *H*? No. University of Georgia, Grambling University, Georgetown University—they all have a *G* for their logo. On my shirt, the bulldog even has a baseball cap with a *G* on it."

"Impressive," said Gwilym.

"I know," Bex agreed.

Bex pulled the car into a parking spot in front of Farrington's Music. Gwilym got out and went into the store, excited to hold his new instrument.

As they entered the store, they saw Joe standing at the counter with a dark-colored, rectangular music case in front of him. He had long gray hair and a couple of missing teeth. He'd been in a rock band when he was younger, but had given it up to open up a music shop.

He smiled at Gwilym. "Here it is, young man!" He tapped the case. "All ready for you."

Gwilym ran his fingers over the top of the case, then opened it and lifted out the instrument. Excitement went through him like lightning. "Wow, it's so—" He turned the trumpet, viewing it from all angles, then pushed the levers down. "Cool."

Joe gave him some care instructions, then Gwilym and Bex thanked him and left the store.

Driving back home, they picked up their game again. Gwilym started off by spotting the logo of Rider University on the back of an SUV. "Who would know that logo unless you went there?"

"Doubtful anyone would. There're hundreds of logos like that, ones that only locals know," said Bex. "Clay thinks Rider's got the best school logo ever."

The back window of the next car came into view with a sticker of the profile of a Native American. "FSU. Buddy's school—and next year by this time you will have already completed a semester there," Gwilym said to his sister. He glanced at her and noticed her slight twitch, prompting him to ask, "So Bex, why haven't you had a boyfriend?"

"Princeton." She pointed to a car ahead of them, avoiding his question. "A *P* with tiger stripes. Another easy one."

Gwilym tried again. "It's just that you're eighteen now and I was wondering why."

"Are you really asking me this? Because, you know, it's none of your business." She sighed and changed her grip on the steering wheel. "I guess I'm just not interested."

"I don't remember you liking anyone. Ever."

"Well, I'm sorry if you think there's something wrong with me," she scoffed. "Maybe I don't want someone to like me. Maybe I don't like the idea of being with someone."

"Plenty of guys like you at school, and you're pretty, smart, and athletic."

"Whatever. Mom didn't seem to need anyone." Their car started up Sourland Mountain.

Gwilym decided not to push her any further. His thoughts went to a mention in one of the letters from his dad of visiting Washington. "Was Dad in Washington?"

"So—that's it about me?" she asked. "What are you asking? Who's from Washington? No one I know of. Grandpa's family is from Baltimore."

"Dad didn't go to college there, did he?"

"No. He went to Rider."

"Oh, I didn't remember that. What about Mom? Where'd she go to college?" The moment the word "Mom" came out of his mouth, he regretted it.

"Mom?" Bex straightened her back. "She went to Princeton."

"I don't know much about her. Other than she's a musician who has a band. No one talks about her." His skin tingled with anticipation of hearing more.

"Maybe we don't talk about her because she left us when we were kids, when you were three years old. Remember?"

"Since it's been ten years, shouldn't I know more about her now?" His growing curiosity about his mom's history was making the decision of whether to meet her easier.

"There's nothing to tell you, Gwilym. She left Princeton after going there for a couple of semesters and left us to start her own band."

"She studied music, right?" His face prickled with warmth.

They pulled into their driveway. "Yes."

"Do you think I'll be good at playing the trumpet?" asked Gwilym. "Do you think I'll have her talent?"

Bex put her hand on his shoulder and squeezed. "Maybe? I'm sure you'll be good at it. You're a Duckworthy. We're all good at something in this family."

"What's Dad good at?"

Bex laughed. "The history of Princeton." Gwilym laughed too.

Once home, Gwilym headed straight to the shed. In the corner, divided off by a square rug Ferguson had bought for him (yesterday, as a surprise), his music studio contained his music stand, stool, record player, records—and now it was complete as he pulled his trumpet from its case. Before attempting his first note, Gwilym put on Coltrane's *Blue Train*, then stood up tall and blew through the mouthpiece. The sound he produced sounded like a dying duck. He laughed. Turning up the sound of Coltrane's trumpet, Gwilym continued blowing into his, imagining he was playing with the jazz master, only stopping from exhaustion and his cheeks hurting. He couldn't wait to begin the lessons that his parents had set up with a music student named Katherine at Rider University. *Eventually, I'll be able to play jazz music with my trumpet in here—my music studio!*

Gwilym had done the fun thing: played his new instrument. Now he had to do the un-fun thing: call his mom. Sitting down on the rug, he crossed his legs. His stomach aching, he tapped on her number. "Mom," he said when he heard her say hello.

"Hello. Gwilym?" Her voice rose in cautious excitement.

He held the phone tight to his face. "Yes—it's me."

"I wasn't sure you'd call me back."

He said, "Well, I thought I should." He dug his fingers into the rug.

"I'm glad you did." Her voice was light and soft. He closed his eyes and listened to her speak. *Do I remember it?* "My band and I are in town for a couple of performances. Princeton invited me back to give two concerts in the University Chapel." He decided that he did have a vague recollection of the sound of her voice.

Focusing on the rug, he brushed his bangs from his eyes. "You said you wanted to meet?" He glanced at his trumpet case. He did want to talk with her about music.

"I thought maybe you'd like to have dinner at Tiger's Tail, like Tigger's tail, right? You loved Tigger. You bounced around like Tigger on his tail when you were a baby."

"It's tale as in fairy tale," he said, remembering now how he liked bouncing like Tigger.

"I wasn't sure. It's been such a long time since I've been in the area."

He didn't say *ten years.*

"We're playing Wednesday and Friday night."

"You're playing at Princeton?" Gwilym said, then added, "Where you studied music?"

"Yes." Her voice raised in volume. He imagined her eyebrows lifting. "Tomorrow would be good for me. Is six o'clock good for you?"

He said yes, hung up, and put the phone in his pocket. *So, that was that.*

He listened to music in his studio that night until he was called in for dinner. Afterward, he went out again. Eventually, his dad came out and reminded him it was getting late.

"This looks great." His dad nodded. "I like the record player. You figured out how to play the records, huh?" He smiled. "Those were your mom's." Gwilym's stomach hurt. "I couldn't get into jazz music. Still don't care for it. In college, Uncle Hal and your mom would listen to it. Your uncle George and I listened to hard rock."

"Like Bex," Gwilym said.

"Right, like Bex." He paused. "I'm sure you'll have your mom's musical talent. I sure don't have any."

Gwilym smiled. "I hope I'm good. I really like these albums. I'm glad you kept them and that the record player still works."

"Glad you're all settled in here. This will be a great place for you to learn the trumpet." He stood looking at Gwilym for a moment, then finally said, "Did you know your mom played the trumpet?"

"Yes."

"I guess I haven't told you much about her."

Gwilym shrugged. "I understand."

"I haven't heard from her since she left. I don't know if your mom has stayed in contact with your aunt Martie or your grandma." Gwilym could see on his dad's face the hurt of having his wife leave him and their kids, pain that Gwilym could only imagine at this point in his life. "Don't stay out here too much longer."

Gwilym watched him walk back to the house. *What would Dad's reaction be if he knew I was meeting her tomorrow night?* His parents' most important rule, the one they expected him and his siblings always to follow, was to be honest. To never lie to them. Trust was also important. They always said, "We trust you. We trust you won't lie to us. We trust you to make good decisions." Gwilym took a big breath and let it out. He didn't want to disappoint his dad and Ferguson by misleading them, but he couldn't tell them, at least not yet, what he was going to do.

MONDAY

Gwilym could make it to Tiger's Tale in twenty minutes on Clay's bike. He looked at himself in the bathroom mirror. He'd run his fingers through his bangs at least a dozen times, but they still didn't sit right for him. Stepping back from the mirror, he tugged at the front of his plaid button-down shirt. It didn't seem to fit right. At least his khaki pants and brown leather tie-up shoes were comfortable. *Geez*. Gwilym was nervous. There was no way around the fact that he wanted to impress his mom by looking sharp. With time to spare, and to calm his nerves, he decided to hang out in the shed and see what noises he could make with the trumpet, and maybe bring another letter to read.

Possibly he would learn something else about his mom before they met tonight.

Gwilym's attempt at producing music with his trumpet was not satisfying to his ears. He wondered if his mom had sounded just as pitiful the first couple of times she'd tried playing. *I hope so.* Resting the trumpet in the case, he sat down and unfolded one of the letters.

> *Nov. 17th*
>
> *C,*
>
> *How are you? I'm okay but I miss you terribly. The past 2 days have been the longest ever. Right now I'm taking a break from my history paper—I hate that class and I hate vegetables. Stupid George has about 15 stupid books, but he says he'll have all As. Anyway . . .*
>
> *Yours, H*

He still was surprised by how funny his dad was. He'd never seemed this silly, but the letters clearly showed his wit. Gwilym had learned other things he didn't know, more about his dad than his mom.

In that first letter, he'd found out his dad wanted to go to music school. He hadn't even known his dad was interested in music. Gwilym was sometimes annoyed when riding in the car with him because of his dad's lackluster taste in music compared to Cat's dad's selections. *I guess I have liked listening to jazz for a while.* And in this letter, there were two more things that didn't make sense: his dad loved reading history books. For example, he would bore Gwilym, Bex, and Clay with details of battles that happened in and around Princeton. Unfortunately for them, living near Princeton gave him way too much history to learn about. Second, his dad loved vegetables, especially Uncle Hal's. Uncle Hal was the one who told Gwilym he hated vegetables, even though he grew the best ones in the county.

Gwilym looked at his watch. *Time to go.* He trotted across the yard and opened the back door to the house. He told his parents goodbye, and that he was going to visit Cat. He didn't like not telling them where he was going. If it wasn't too late, maybe he'd stop by Cat's for just a minute on the way back. The only problem was when they asked him why he was dressed up. He lied to them a second time, explaining he had to give a speech at school and he wanted to see if Cat liked the outfit he was planning to wear. *Wow. That was a dumb excuse!*

When Gwilym pulled up in front of the restaurant on his bike, his stomach ached. *I don't know if I'll be able to eat.* He loved their burgers and peach cobbler. *Maybe I can manage a burger.* He looked around the outside for a bike rack. He hadn't thought ahead about protecting Clay's bike and hadn't brought a lock. "Where am I going to put it?"

"Gwilym?" Without turning, he recognized the voice.

"Mom?" He blushed. He sounded like such a kid.

"Do you want to put your bike in my car? It should fit." She was standing next to a big SUV with the back open.

He hesitated, trying to identify this new sensation—that she would take care of him. He felt nervous again. "Thanks. I didn't think about how I was going to lock it up."

As they walked into the restaurant and the waitress showed them to their table, Gwilym told his mom about his lost bike. While they waited on their food, she told him about the time one of her favorite trumpets was stolen. He asked if she got it back. She did, eventually.

She wore a maroon sweater that looked very soft and had a bow on one shoulder. She slouched slightly and as she talked her long arms and fingers moved constantly, like she was playing an imaginary instrument.

The dinner went more smoothly than Gwilym had expected. He slurped his soda and munched on his burger and fries. They talked about Clay's job at Rider University's library, and Bex getting a softball scholarship from FSU. When they talked about his sister, he noticed his mother's expression changed, her brow furrowed.

"She was really mad at me for leaving you all. It was very hurtful when she started calling herself Bex. I hoped she'd go back to Beth, since it *is* Grandma's name. Do you remember the sign she made? It said 'My name is no longer Beth! It is BeX' with a big *X* over the *th*. She taped it to her bedroom door!"

Gwilym knew this story, of course, but he didn't like his mom's tone when she was talking about his sister. It made him uncomfortable. After all, *she* was the one who'd left *them.* So how could she be surprised by Bex's actions? His arms and hands felt prickly. He wanted to leave—now. He glanced at the two unoccupied chairs at the table, wishing he'd asked Bex or Clay, or both, to come with him tonight.

"What time is it?" He looked at his phone. "I've got to go. They'll be wondering why I'm not back yet." He scooted out his chair, stood up, and threw on his jacket. His mom waved at the waitress to bring the check. "Thanks for dinner—" He couldn't get "Mom" to come out of his mouth.

"Gwilym." She reached for his arm. "I'd like you, Bex, and Clay to come to my band's performances." She pushed three tickets into his hand. He took them and stuffed both hands into his jacket pockets.

A heat wave swept across his chest. "Don't you think you should call them first? To talk to them?" he stammered. "You don't seriously expect me to tell them. They don't even know I'm having dinner with you."

The waitress brought the check and took the credit card his mom had ready. "I—" She looked down at her hands and told Gwilym, "I didn't know what to do, honestly."

Her shoulders slumped and she said quietly, "Please, Gwilym. I only worked up the nerve to see the three of you last week."

"Last week." Gwilym lowered his voice when the waitress returned with the receipt. After she walked away, Gwilym continued, "You only decided to see your kids last week, after abandoning them ten years ago? A last-minute thought. 'Oh, I'd almost forgotten my kids live near Princeton. Maybe I should contact them. Because I'm sure they'd want to see me.'" He wasn't surprised that his mom was thinking only of herself.

She took the napkin from her lap, pushed back her chair, and stood facing Gwilym. His cheeks flushed as she seemed to loom over him. "I know," she said. "You can't understand."

"I'm tired. I want to go home." He turned to walk out of the restaurant. She followed. When they got to the parking lot, he said without looking at her, "I need my bike."

She opened the back of the SUV. When Gwilym reached in to pull out the bike, she leaned in to help. "I can do it," he said quietly. He thanked her again for dinner. Then he pushed off onto the dark road. He pedaled as hard as he could, until the muscles in his calves ached the way his heart did. The wind spread his tears across his face as he ascended Sourland Mountain.

His parents were sitting on the couch watching TV when Gwilym charged into the house, and he suddenly realized he'd forgotten to stop at Cat's. "Sorry I'm late. I lost track of time."

"Okay, love," said Ferguson.

"I don't even know what time it is," his dad added.

Since they didn't seem concerned, Gwilym felt relieved that he'd managed to get away with his lies. He said good night and headed upstairs. As he climbed the steps, his feet felt like bricks. The door to his sister's room was open. She was slouched on her bed, reading one of her English literature books. He stepped inside and closed the door behind him. Like with Aunt Martie, he'd get the words out.

"Bex, I had dinner with Mom."

"When?" She sat up.

"Tonight."

"Where?"

"I met her at Tiger's Tale."

She pulled her ponytail. "No wonder you look such a mess." She moved her legs so he could sit next to her. She stared at him. "I don't understand. You went to dinner with her tonight. That means it was a prearranged thing, which means you talked to her—when?"

"*She* called *me* on Thanksgiving Day in the middle of the scavenger hunt."

"What? And you didn't tell me?"

"I didn't know it was her. I let the call go to voice mail because the number came up as an unknown caller. She left a message, but I didn't listen to it until Friday. I just called her back yesterday."

"And this is Monday night," Bex said. "And again, you're just now telling me you had dinner with our mom." She stood up and huffed.

"She asked to meet me." Why did he sound like he was defending *her*?

Bex circled her room. "Do you think she's going to call me? No, no. She doesn't have my number. Wait, how does she have yours? Has she called Clay, do you think? No, he would have immediately told us. Unless she made him promise not to."

"Stop pacing, Bex. Please."

"How'd she get your number?" she asked again.

He hesitated. "From Aunt Martie."

"Of course! She's been spying on us all these years."

"She's our aunt, and she helped raise us, Bex," he said quietly.

She shook her head and paced faster. "So you've been with our mom, and you didn't tell me."

"I'm telling you now! What could I do? *She* asked *me* to meet her."

"Say *no*?" Bex's eyes were wide with anger. He didn't like that look.

"I couldn't." He stared down at his hands.

"Of course not." She sat on the bed beside him. "You're too freaking polite. Why's she here?"

"Her band's playing on the Princeton campus Wednesday and Friday night this week."

"The Caroline McCorkle Band," she said sarcastically. "I remember the name. Well, as long as it's convenient for her. Well!" She crossed her arms, then asked, "How was it?"

"It seemed almost normal for a while, which was weird because I haven't seen her since I was three. It felt like a regular dinner, like other parents and kids have."

"Only you were there with *our* mom, the woman who left, as you said, when you were three." She stood up again and pointed a thumb at her chest. "I was only eight. Clay was ten. What mom does that to her kids?"

"So you're not mad at me?" He looked at her pleadingly.

"No. Better you than me." She sat back down on the bed.

"Will you go to the concerts with me? She gave me the tickets."

"I hate jazz." She leaned back on the headboard. "Why would she call you instead of me?" Her eyes were shining with tears.

"I thought you were glad she didn't call you." He knew that wasn't true.

"I lied." She looked at the ceiling. "Well, anyway, I know why. She knows I would hang up on her." She sat up straight and smiled. "I would answer and then when I heard her voice I'd hang up on her."

"Who would you hang up on?" Clay asked. He'd opened the door so quietly they hadn't noticed he'd come in. His brows were scrunched together and his eyes looked glassy.

"I didn't see you come in, Clay." Gwilym swallowed hard. "You know who we're talking about, don't you?"

Clay immediately turned around and headed back out the door.

"Please stop, Clay. Don't walk away," Gwilym said.

"We were coming to tell you, Clay," said Bex. "We're sorry if it seems like we were hiding this from you, but I just found out too!"

Clay came back in the room, wringing his hands. "I want Mom to see where I work."

"If that's what you want, Clay," Gwilym said. "I'll tell her you want her to come to the library."

"Wait. Are you supposed to call her again?" Bex asked.

"I guess." Gwilym lifted his shoulders. "She wants us to go to the concerts. She never said she'd call you or Clay. I don't *want* to call her, but I guess I have to."

"I'll call her," Bex said. "Give me her number." Bex was holding her phone.

"But you just said you didn't want to talk to her."

"Well, I probably should since . . ." She glanced sideways at Clay.

Clay stared at the floor, his hands in his pockets. "I want to see Mom."

Gwilym tilted his head. "Clay, aren't you mad at Mom for leaving us?"

"She had to go away," he explained. "She plays in a jazz band and she has to travel with them all over the world. She's in charge of the band."

Bex shrugged at Gwilym. "There's your answer."

"Are you going to call her?" Gwilym saw she was hesitating. "You don't have to. I'll—"

"Yes, I know," Bex snapped, then rubbed her forehead. "She makes me so mad."

He moved closer to her on the bed. "Let's not call her now. It's only going to upset you more and you'll probably say something you'll regret."

"Yeah, well." Bex set the phone down beside her. "Where would we start the conversation? 'So, Mom, you've been gone some time now . . . What's new?'"

Gwilym didn't say he'd just talked about what he'd been doing. That it was like meeting up with someone you haven't seen in a long time. Although, this was their mom they were talking about.

"You call her," Bex said to Gwilym. "You tell her we'll come to her *jazz* concerts."

"It'll be okay," Clay reassured her.

She took his hand. "It will be, with you two with me."

TUESDAY

Another weekday morning with the house full of commotion. Dad was in the hallway ironing his shirt. Bex was yelling at Clay to get out of the bathroom. Ferguson was blow-drying her hair in their bathroom. Gwilym heard all of this from inside his room, tucked in bed with the door open a crack. He felt protected and safe—and happy at the sounds of the people in his house. All these things, and yet, he felt a weariness inside him. He picked up the letter from his nightstand that he'd selected last night to read this morning.

May 6th

C,

How are you? Today me and George bought our books. I only have one: Theater 3000. On another topic: I think George's got a crush on your sister. He's acting really pathetic around her lately . . .

Gwilym thought about what he knew about his dad—and wondered now if these letters were from him. This letter was signed *Yours,* like the other two. His dad had said in the shed that he didn't listen to jazz music. Had he been a good student? Gwilym didn't know. And *Theater 3000? Did my dad mean* Mystery Science Theater 3000*? I bet he did. I wonder if Mom got the joke.* Thinking about his mom made Gwilym tired. Talking to her on the phone, seeing her, made his head feel foggy this morning. He'd read one of the letters hoping it would cheer him up. But it hadn't. The letter rested on his stomach. He inhaled, but could only move the air into his chest, not into his belly for a deep breath—it felt like there was a boulder pressing down on him.

I can't go to school today. There's no way I can do it. I don't feel like I can do anything. Gwilym turned onto his side and put his hand on his stomach. Sadness overtook him. *What's happening to me?* A panic spread though him. *Great.* One of the dogs walked down the hallway. Baby pushed his way into Gwilym's room. The cinnamon-colored dog jumped onto the bed and sank his head onto the comforter, snorted, and closed his eyes. Gwilym petted him and pulled up the covers.

"Gwilym. *Gwilym?*" Ferguson peered into his room. "Are you up?" She looked concerned.

"I don't think I can go to school today." His mind was still cloudy.

"You don't feel well?" asked his stepmom.

"No." He balled up the sheets.

"Okay. I'll call you later to see how you're feeling."

"Okay," said Gwilym. "Thanks." He shut his eyes, listening to the door click shut.

He heard his parents murmuring. Then his dad yelled up to him, "Feel better, Gwilym." The garage door closed and a moment later the cars started.

Instead of feeling safe and warm under his covers, the sound of his parents leaving and the realization that he was alone in the house made him feel sad again. This time he wasn't missing school because he was sick. His body ached, but not like it did when he had the flu. He had the sensation of sinking through the mattress, through the box spring, through the floor, all the way to the ground where he would lie forever. Like a large rock, unable to move. He moved his legs to make sure he could, disturbing Baby. The dog resettled himself, and Gwilym petted him again. "Thanks, Baby, for staying with me."

He went back to sleep and dreamed he was watching his mom at Uncle Hal's stand again. This time Uncle Hal kissed his mom's cheek. When he woke up he looked at the clock on his bedside table. Only an hour had gone by. He began feeling uneasy. As he lay in bed, the uncomfortable feeling changed into fear. And, he thought, not the anxiety of failing a test, but an overwhelming sensation that nothing would be right again—that he would never have a happy life again. *I feel so unhappy.* Tears ran down his cheeks when he closed his eyes.

He woke up, not aware that he'd fallen asleep again. His anxiety wasn't as intense now, and he realized, *I'm bored!*

Gwilym looked at the book on his bedside table, *It's Like This, Cat,* by Emily Cheney Neville. It had won the Newbery Medal, a big-time award for children's literature. He'd read it about a hundred times. He'd read it again today. He liked the story because the main character, Dave, has a cat he names Cat. Baby and Bear were the only pets his family had had since he was a baby. Gwilym thought that someday he'd like to have a cat, too. Right now the only Cat he was around was his best friend Cat.

Each time he read the book, certain details would jump out at him—probably, he thought, based on what was going on in his life at the time. Sometimes it took him out of the story and he'd have to make himself get back to reading it. Like today—he didn't get past page three before he was staring at the ceiling. Gwilym laughed at the very first sentence. He hadn't thought the first sentence was funny until reading it at this moment. Dave gets a cat because he knows it'll make his dad roar! Gwilym could see Bex doing the same thing to their parents, if they provoked her like Dave's dad. But their parents were tame compared with the fictional parent, so Bex just acted like she was annoyed most of the time. The second bit of the story that stopped him was on page three, where Dave's dad "hisses" at him that he's upsetting his mom. Gwilym thought of Cat and the recent trouble she'd had in her family. He remembered her telling him that Buddy had yelled the same thing at her when she'd raced out their front door in her wheelchair and almost crashed onto the cement walkway.

He was pulled out of that thought by Baby scratching at the door. "Can't you take yourself out?" The dog wagged its tail. "All right." He got out of bed. Wearing a T-shirt and pajama bottoms, he followed the dog down the stairs. Bear was waiting at the front door.

Gwilym sat on the edge of the front stoop with his feet in the grass and closed his eyes, feeling the sun on his face. Listening to Baby and Bear walking around the yard, Gwilym didn't move until a dog's wet nose nuzzled his hand. "You're done now?" He opened his eyes and rubbed Baby's head. "You too, Bear?"

Back in bed, he opened the book and read for a bit, then slept. He woke up to the sound of a car pulling into the driveway, then one of his parents climbing the stairs.

"Are you feeling better?" his dad asked, sitting on the edge of the bed.

"A little bit." Gwilym was leaning against his pillow, his legs stretched out.

Gwilym got up and followed his dad into the kitchen. The rest of his family was arriving home. The regular evening routine was beginning. After dinner he felt like himself again. He didn't understand what had happened to him. Why he had felt so bad inside his head. *Weird.*

❧

That night in bed when Gwilym was finishing *It's Like This, Cat,* lightning flashed outside his window. He paused in his reading and counted the seconds until he heard the thunder. It was followed by the sound of rain thumping against the roof. He looked at the dark sky, then noticed a glow reflecting at the bottom of his window. He got up and looked down at the shed. He gasped. It was on fire!

Gwilym ran into his parents' bedroom. "Dad! The shed was struck by lightning! It's on fire!" He heard a mumble and then the covers being thrown off. "I'll call 911!" he heard Ferguson say.

He ran downstairs and out to the shed, panicking because he didn't know what to do.

His dad shouted, "Help me with the hose, Gwilym!" They stretched it as far as it would go. But it was attached to the spigot on the opposite side of the house, so it couldn't reach the shed. "Get a bucket from the garage and start filling it up." Gwilym obeyed his dad.

Bex, Ferguson, and Clay followed with buckets. They threw the water onto the fire, but it didn't slow it. Fortunately, the fire didn't jump to any trees around the building.

The family stopped filling their buckets and stood side by side watching the small building burn. *So many family memories in there.*

Bex wrapped her arm around her dad's waist. "It's all gone. Everything." He put his arms around her and Gwilym. Clay leaned against Ferguson.

"Our baby albums . . ." Clay said.

"Grandpa's tackle box," said Bex.

"No. I have that in my bedroom," Gwilym told her. *And the letters.*

"How come you have it—" She gasped. "Your trumpet, Gwilym."

Gwilym's eyes locked on the flames. *No, no, no. My trumpet. And the records and record player.* He smudged tears from his cheeks.

"I'm so sorry." Ferguson put her arm around him. "Here's the fire truck. Let's get out of the way." She kissed the top of his head. "We'll get you another trumpet. Don't worry about it."

"What's most important," said his dad, "is we are okay." He walked to the driveway to meet the firemen.

"Let's go inside," suggested Ferguson. "I'll make some coffee." They followed her into the kitchen.

Before going inside, Gwilym breathed in the combination of cold air and the burning wood of the shed. The smell reminded him of his grandma's cigarettes. He sighed. Would he be able to enjoy sitting with her as she smoked? Would the smell just remind him of the shed that was gone, along with the important things inside it? His trumpet, the records and record player, their baby albums . . .

It didn't take the firemen long to douse the fire. As he rested his arms on the counter, he listened to the fire truck back out of the driveway. He thought of the photographs of everybody's favorite things still on their phones from the scavenger hunt. Those things hadn't been destroyed in the fire. Bex had her turquoise mermaid drink stirrer; Clay had his John Denver poster. The only things he had were the letters and the tackle box. No bike, no trumpet. *The trumpet.* He imagined Joe's disappointed face after he learned what happened to it. *What's going to happen? Will he let me rent another trumpet?* Panic ran through him. *What if I can't get a trumpet and can't learn to play jazz or play in the school band? Why is everything so hard right now?* He took a big swig of the steaming coffee, almost choking on the hot liquid as it went down his throat, then he got up and poured the rest down the sink. It was six o'clock in the morning. He wanted to go to school and see Hattie and Cat. "I'll get ready for school."

WEDNESDAY

Gwilym had been glad to see Hattie and Cat at school, but he felt melancholy all day. While riding home from school on Clay's bike, he pulled up next to Hattie, who was getting the mail out of her mailbox.

She immediately told him that she was sorry about what had happened to the shed. Then she asked, "So, you're going to see your mom play in her band tonight?"

"How'd you know that?"

"I heard my mom talking about it to my dad."

"How'd she know?" *I guess Mom called Aunt Martie again.* "Did you hear me and your mom talking the other day?"

"Yes," she said. She kicked some gravel on her driveway.

"I'm sorry I didn't tell you."

"It's okay," said Hattie. "It must be really hard right now with your mom here and everything else."

"Yeah, well, not much I can do about my bike or the shed."

"I hope you enjoy the concert tonight." She smiled at her cousin and headed up her driveway.

Gwilym pedaled up his driveway and trudged into the house. His parents' cars weren't in the garage. Clay was sitting at the kitchen table reading a textbook; Bex was leaning against the sink counter drinking a glass of water. Gwilym swung his backpack onto a chair and sat next to Clay.

"I don't feel like going to the concert tonight." Gwilym avoided looking out the window at the black spot where the shed had been.

"No. It's really not what I'd pick to do tonight." Bex downed the water.

"And we didn't tell Dad or Ferguson," Gwilym added. "Do you think we should?"

"We probably should tell them about Friday's concert. We'll tell them we have to go to the university library tonight. That you have to find some books for class," said Bex.

"Okay," Gwilym agreed reluctantly. *Another lie.*

Clay concentrated on his reading. Gwilym and Bex locked eyes.

"How you doing, Clay?" Gwilym asked.

"Yeah, Clay. How are you doing?" Bex added.

Clay finished reading a sentence, then looked up with watery eyes. "That's lying. It's against the rules."

"I know, Clay," said Bex. "But sometimes we have to tell a lie." She looked at Gwilym for help.

"Yeah, Clay. We can't just spring all this on them right now."

"Why not?" Clay asked simply.

"Because," explained Bex, "it's a lot to throw at them. And we don't have time tonight to sit down with them to explain everything that's happened. We can't tell them as we're running out the door. Don't you agree?" She put her hand on his shoulder.

Clay lowered his head. "We're not supposed to lie to our parents."

"We know, Clay," said Gwilym. "But . . ." Bex signaled to him to let it go.

❧

"I can't believe we're going to see Mom tonight," said Bex with her hands on her hips. "Ten years, and now we're going to her concert."

"Yeah," said Gwilym. They were standing with Clay inside his bedroom, where a mellow John Denver song was playing that didn't fit the mood of the three listeners.

They walked downstairs and into the kitchen. Gwilym had volunteered to tell Dad and Ferguson their plan. *Might as well continue the lies.*

"What's up?" asked his stepmom. "You guys seem a bit gloomy tonight."

"Yeah," said Bex. Gwilym looked at her. "Well, your son here"—she pointed at him—"just let us know he has a report on native birds due tomorrow, and the assignment includes taking out books from the library."

"I forgot," Gwilym said, hoping he looked sheepish.

"And I forgot a book for my class, so we have to go to the university library." Gwilym and Bex looked at Clay. "And then we have to—" Gwilym fought off a smile.

"Yes, that's good, Clay. They get it," said Bex, putting a hand on his arm. She turned to their parents. "We'll try not to be too late."

❧

Bex found a parking spot near the main entrance to Princeton University. As the three approached the gate, Gwilym heard his dad's voice: "What we are walking through is the FitzRandolph Gate, built in 1905." Gwilym thought it was impressive, with the ornate metalwork set around the university crest, and the two stone columns topped with eagles with their wings spread. He and his siblings crossed the campus to the University Chapel, where the concert would be held tonight and Friday night. Again, Gwilym heard his dad say, "This chapel was built between 1925 and 1928. It is one of the most beautiful Gothic buildings in the US *and* the third largest college church in the world."

The darkness had almost completely covered the stone buildings they walked past, the warm light coming from the windows making them look like they were on fire. The glow brought the image of the shed fire back to him. But then it was replaced with an image of his mom and her band jamming. Gwilym was excited for his first time seeing his mom play the trumpet. He was going to hear live jazz! As they entered the chapel, large columns rose around them, adding to the importance of the event, and lit candles made it even more special. An usher greeted them and directed them to their assigned seats three rows from the front of the church, where three microphones and a drum set had been placed.

Bex entered the row, then Gwilym and Clay.

"These are impressive seats," said Bex.

"They are," agreed Gwilym, and Clay nodded.

Waiting for the performance to begin, Gwilym observed the stained glass windows, amazed by how they'd maintained their intense colors for so long. Bex got up and said she was going to use the bathroom before the concert started; Clay sat reading the program.

Half an hour later, the three band members walked out from a side door in the chapel and took their positions in front of the audience, who clapped enthusiastically. Standing in front of the microphone was their mom, in a shiny, emerald-colored dress, holding her trumpet. On either side of her were her bassist and drummer, wearing fancy suits. Gwilym wanted to wear a stylish suit like theirs someday when he played in a jazz band. Already he was envisioning this image of himself, even though he hadn't played a note on a trumpet yet!

"Good evening!" The audience clapped again. "I'm Caroline and this is the Caroline McCorkle Band." More clapping and cheering. "Thank you." Gwilym noticed her pause. *Is she going to say we're here?* "Tonight," she continued. "Tonight is a special night." Bex bumped Gwilym's arm and Clay sat up tall in his seat. "My children are in the audience. I won't ask them to stand up, but they are the three beautiful people sitting there in the middle of the third row." She pointed to them and the spotlight swung around to shine on them. Enormous applause followed. "I'm blessed," she continued. "I have traveled the world. I have had an amazing career. It keeps amazing me." She stopped. "But as you can imagine, this has not come without sacrifices." She smiled at Gwilym and his siblings.

Gwilym had broken out in a sweat. Bex put her hand on his and squeezed. He glanced at her, but she was staring up at their mom, obviously not enjoying this moment either. *We'll get through this,* he wanted to say to Bex. *Start your set, please, Mom.* But she kept talking. Something about having to give up moments of her children's lives. Gwilym turned to Clay. His brother's face had a serious expression Gwilym rarely saw. *Oh, please stop talking, Mom.*

"Well, enough of this sentimentality. Now, almost as important, are my band members," she said with a wink. "On drums, Joshua Riley, and my bassist, Christian McGannon! A-one-two-three-four."

And the band played.

And did his mom's band play!

They were the best jazz band Gwilym had ever heard, live or recorded—forgetting that he hadn't heard a live jazz band until now. His feet tapped to the beat. *Wow. If I could be even a tiny bit as good as my mom and her band.* The sound of the music seemed to swirl around the stage, around each band member, in and out of their instruments. Then came his mom's solo. Gwilym teared up from the intensity of the notes. He hadn't expected that listening to the band would be so emotional. Bex patted his hand.

Gwilym wiped his cheeks. He wished he could go to the privacy of the bathroom to dry his eyes, but climbing over the others in their row would just draw more attention to himself. He was pretty sure Bex had a tissue in her small pink-flowered purse, but he appreciated her sparing him further embarrassment by not offering him one.

The jam session ended, followed by tremendous applause and thank-yous from the band members.

"Yeah, all right!" Gwilym yelled.

Clay shouted, "Whoa-whoa!" and Bex clapped.

Their mom and her band bowed, then headed back into the side room.

The concert had lasted over two hours. The three got up from their seats, their legs stiff. Bex and Clay looked as exhausted and exhilarated as Gwilym felt. They followed the crowd flowing out into the lobby.

"Well?" asked Gwilym, for he was the only true jazz enthusiast in the family. "What'd you think?"

"Almost as good as John Denver." Clay smiled.

"I'd like to see them play with Metallica," Bex announced.

Gwilym grew apprehensive as several passing groups recognized them as Caroline's children. "You must be proud!" one guy said, giving them a thumbs-up. Bex and Clay looked hesitant to accept the accolades, but said, "Thanks."

As the crowd thinned, Bex wrapped her arm around Gwilym's shoulders. "What do you think? Are we supposed to go and say hi?" she asked.

Gwilym shrugged. "I guess so."

"Let's go then," she said, looking nervous.

"Wait." Gwilym stopped them. "Tell me Bex, jazz isn't too bad, is it?"

Bex laughed. "I never would have gone to a jazz concert by choice. I guess it wasn't too bad."

Gwilym turned to his brother. "Should we go see her?"

"Yes," said Clay.

They walked into the room where the band had gone to find only Joshua and Christian packing up their instruments.

"Hi, I'm Gwilym . . ." He hesitated. "Caroline's son." Saying those words felt strange. "And this is my sister, Bex, and my brother, Clay. We're here to see our mom."

"I'm Christian," said the bassist, shaking their hands.

"Oh, yes. Nice to meet you." The drummer shook hands. "I'm Joshua." He turned to Bex. "I've heard about the beautiful daughter." She blushed. "Your mom asked us to apologize to you. Something came up—not an emergency, but she had something she had to take care of. So she had to leave. She said for you to call her later."

The siblings stood, awkwardly watching the musicians finish packing up their remaining things, say good night, then leave.

Gwilym was the first to snap out of his shock. "Christian is coming back."

Christian had walked back through the door. He was carrying an instrument case. "I almost forgot. Here." He handed Gwilym the case. "Your mom left this for you. It's the first trumpet she owned. She played it all over Europe on our first tour there. She wanted you to have it. She said you probably already have your own, but now you have two! See you Friday!" He went back out the door.

Gwilym stared at the case in his hand.

"Well, open it!" said Bex.

He balanced it on a seat and clicked it open. The trumpet shone, surrounded by what appeared to be black velvet cushioning.

"Great timing," said Bex.

"Now you don't have to get another one," said Clay.

Gwilym stared at the trumpet in his hand. *I have Mom's trumpet. She gave me her trumpet.* It must be the one she'd talked about at the restaurant. His arms and legs felt shaky.

THURSDAY

On Gwilym's ride home from school, still on Clay's bike, he passed by the produce stand. Uncle Hal motioned him to stop. "Hey, could you drop this off on your way home?" Gwilym secured the basket with the tag "Hamilton" on it, then texted Cat, who was already home.

"Hi." Cat was sitting in her wheelchair next to the kitchen table. "My uncle's keeping you busy." She twisted her braid.

"Yes." Gwilym put the basket on the counter and sat down in a chair at the table. "Did you say you're going to get your casts off next week?"

"Yes!" Her eyes brightened. "Next week. I can't believe it! It feels like I've been in these casts and wheelchair forever."

"And then you'll start physical therapy?"

"Yes. Buddy went through physical therapy a couple of years ago, when he hurt his knee. I'm going to the same place."

"He liked it, right?" She nodded.

They were silent for a moment. "So . . ." Gwilym began. "I haven't talked with you since the Thanksgiving football game. I got a call from my mom."

Cat frowned. "Your mom? But, I thought, I mean, when was the last time you saw her? She left when you were a baby, didn't she?"

"Yeah. I had dinner with her at Tiger's Tale, which went okay, but not great. And then last night Bex, Clay, and I saw her and her band play at the University Chapel."

"Wow. Was she good?"

"Yes. We didn't see her afterward, but they have another concert Friday that we're going to. All these things are happening at once. My bike disappearing, my mom coming into town, and now, listen to this: You know we lost everything that was in the shed in the fire. My trumpet that I was renting is ruined. Well, last night she gave me her trumpet, I mean one of her trumpets, one she played all over Europe!"

"Wow," Cat said again. "Does your dad know she's here?"

"No. Not yet."

"Are you going to tell him?"

"We're going to have to let him and Ferguson know *very soon,* since the concert's tomorrow night."

"I'd say so," agreed Cat. "What do you think your dad will say?"

"Well, he'll be mad that we lied to him and Ferguson, that's for sure. But other than punishing me for who knows how long, I don't know what he'll say."

"Hey, what are you doing right now? I'm going to Benton's studio. I want to show him my sketches. You want to come with me? It'd take your mind off talking to your parents."

"Okay." Gwilym nodded.

Cat smiled. "You can roll me there."

"I figured." He took the handles of the wheelchair and they headed to Benton's studio. Benton

Whitman (a relative of the American poet Walt Whitman) was a landscape painter. He rented the barn-turned-art studio on Cat's family's land, which also included her family's house, her uncle's place, and his market stand.

"Hi, Benton," said Cat. "Mind if Gwilym and I disturb you? I wanted to show you my drawings."

"Come in. I need a break from this piece." Benton laid down his paintbrush and examined his work, then nodded. He was dressed in a button-down denim shirt and dark jeans. Benton had thick, wavy, golden-brown hair and a mustache and beard with a few white stripes. His hair flared out at his neck so that from the top of his head to his neck looked like a triangle. Gwilym chuckled, thinking how Cat described her uncle as having a rectangle head because of his cropped haircut.

Cat had begun taking drawing lessons from Benton when he moved in. Cat had confided in Gwilym that the companionship had helped her deal with her mom's depression, which had developed after the trauma of the car crash. *Art and healing.* Cat told him that learning to draw had helped her to deal with her feelings. He wondered if music could help someone deal with difficult emotions. It was an idea that he wanted to learn more about.

"Let me see your drawings, Cat." Benton flipped through her small sketchbook. "Very nice. I like this tree here." He outlined the shape of the object with his finger, then tilted his head toward Gwilym. "Cat and I are going to visit the tree their car hit."

"In the summer," added Cat. "I don't want to go now in the cold weather."

"It might be more challenging for you to draw the tree and the surrounding ones when they are covered in green foliage." He returned the book to his student, then said to Gwilym, "I heard you playing your trumpet."

Gwilym was embarrassed at the sounds Benton must have heard. "I don't think you can call what's been coming out of my trumpet music. I haven't started taking lessons yet."

"Gwilym just got a new trumpet, since the one he rented was damaged in the shed fire. It was his mom's trumpet!" Cat said. Benton told Gwilym that was wonderful.

Gwilym was envious of Benton living next door to Cat. "If a jazz musician lived with us, I could take music lessons like you take art lessons."

"You know, Gwilym," Benton said, "the arts intermingle. They work together, influence each other all the time."

Gwilym sat on a stool next to Cat. "What do you mean?"

"For example, jazz." Benton jumped off his seat and walked over to a long bookcase across the back wall. He scanned the books. "Here." He pulled out a small rectangular book: *Jazz,* by Henri Matisse. "Did any of your classmates do an art report on Henri Matisse?"

Gwilym's eyes widened. It was the picture on the cover of Wynton Marsalis's *The Majesty of the Blues.*

"Have you seen the picture before?" Cat asked.

"Yeah. It's on the cover of one of the jazz albums I was listening to the other day."

"Wow. That's a coincidence," his friend remarked.

Gwilym looked at it closely. On the left side was a block of bright yellow, on the right an equally bold blue. *University of Michigan colors.* Three cursive words were on the yellow side: "Henri Matisse" and "Jazz." The black cutout figure on the cover had its arms raised and its feet parted. It looked like it had been created by a child. Where its heart would be was a small red dot. The color matched the word "jazz." *Heart-Love-Jazz.* "I like the way the yellow stars float around the figure. They look like a child made them." Gwilym opened the book. "They're cutouts! Cool! Here you go, here's a quote about a tree for you, Cat. 'No leaf of a fig tree is identical with any other of its leaves, each has a form of its own but they all proclaim: Fig tree!'"

"Hmm," said Cat. "Maybe we should go see the tree in winter when the leaves are down."

Benton laughed. "You would think so, Cat. Gwilym, why don't you go get your trumpet? I have an idea."

Gwilym read to himself: *Jazz. The images, in vivid and violent tones, have resulted from crystallizations of memories . . .* "Huh? I'm sorry. What did you say?"

Benton repeated what he'd said.

Gwilym handed the book to Cat. "Be right back." As he left the barn, he heard her say, "I've seen posters of these." He ran to his house, excited by whatever Benton's idea would be.

Returning with his trumpet, Gwilym awaited Benton's idea. His trumpet rested under his arm.

"Pick an image you like," the artist instructed.

Gwilym balanced the little book on the stool. Some images had a circus theme; some figures were dancing. He was not one to dance. "Here." He held up the one he chose.

"It's a monster," said Cat. "I like it."

"What does it look like to you, Gwilym?"

The image had sections of solid green, blue, fuchsia, and orange. Blue and fuchsia made up the largest areas of color around the white head of a "monster," maybe a dog? The mouth was a shape Gwilym interpreted as angry, but it also looked like it could be laughing. Its red eye didn't reveal what the being was feeling. Its ear was flopped over the way Baby's or Bear's folded when they were angry, or when they were happy because he was petting them. Gwilym frowned. "It looks like my dogs, Baby and Bear. I can't decide if he looks mad or happy, though."

"Does he have to be one or the other?" Benton asked.

"No, I guess not." He took his trumpet from under his arm.

"Play what Baby or Bear would sound like if they were mad."

Gwilym put the mouthpiece to his lips and blew. A low, deep sound emerged from the instrument. Then the note rose higher and higher into a roar, or a howl. Then quick notes sounded like barks. He took the trumpet away from his lips and looked to the other two for their reactions.

"I can see Baby," said Cat. "I can see him barking and whining at you because he doesn't have his food. Or he's barking at a squirrel tormenting him."

Benton nodded. "I could see it too. Now, why don't you play what Baby or Bear would sound like if they were happy."

Gwilym played quick, middle-volume notes. Then he made the trumpet sound like laughter.

"I like the mad Baby. The notes you played for that made me see it better," said Cat.

"Maybe happy is harder to play," suggested Benton. "But you're getting the idea. What we're trying here is called synesthesia. Remember the word, Cat?"

"No," said Cat.

"I thought we talked about it with the colors you saw when you hit the tree."

"Definitely not. I would have remembered that."

"Okay, then let's have the discussion now. When your car hit the tree—"

Gwilym cringed.

Benton continued. "Did you see any colors when you felt your legs break?"

With her eyes closed, Cat sat motionless, then said, "I remember an image of my legs swaying back and forth like swings as my bones broke." She opened her eyes. "I saw red and a bluish purple. Yes, I remember the dark dashboard, the car headlights on the tree trunk, and those colors."

"And that was before you would have seen any lights from the police or emergency vehicles," Gwilym said. "Did they look like the shapes of the colors in the Matisse picture?"

"No. They were flashing. Like two flashlights shining on where we hit."

"What is synth-tes-ia?" Gwilym asked Benton.

"Sin-es-thee-zhuh is when a person experiences two different senses at the same time—when one sense, like sound, jolts another sense, like sight. Or in Cat's experience, feel or touch and sight. But this is how we can combine art with music: the visual to the audible."

"I think I understand," said Gwilym.

"I don't," blurted Cat.

"I think Benton's saying when you felt your legs break you saw colors."

"Cool," said Cat. "Maybe the colors came into my mind to try to calm me."

"I like the idea. Interesting. I haven't heard this analysis before," Benton said.

"I hadn't thought of playing a work of art," said Gwilym.

"Choose another page," suggested Benton.

Gwilym pointed. "I like this wild one." He held up the book, and they took in the image of an orange border with beige, green, and yellow squares. Matisse had cut tiny black squares, maybe fifty of them, and placed them on the yellow; then the same color was accompanied by blue, fuchsia, and dark orange squiggles. "I see these squiggles are on many of Matisse's cutouts that we've looked at."

"What sounds would you hear coming from that one?" asked Benton.

"May I?" asked Cat. Benton nodded. "I hear shouts and squeaks."

"Where in the composition do you hear these sounds?" asked Benton.

"The shouts would be from the two rectangular pieces at the top of the picture." She took the book from Gwilym and put it in her lap. "And the squeaks come from the squiggles in blue and orange and fuchsia. Or those cute little black squares. Maybe they're the ones squeaking."

"The rectangles could represent trumpets," Gwilym suggested. "And they're blurting out the ton of small black squares." He raised the instrument to his lips, but quickly lowered it. "I want to think about this one before playing random notes."

"Jazz, like any great art, only appears to be spontaneous." Benton smiled. "You may borrow this book, if you'd like to," he offered.

"Thank you. I'll try looking at the pictures and matching sounds when I have some free time."

"C'mon, Gwilym. Take me back home. *Please.*"

"Thanks for the visit." Benton waved as they went out the studio-barn door.

FRIDAY

Tonight was his mom's second performance. Gwilym was dressed in a plaid button-down shirt, khaki pants, and brown leather tie-up shoes. It was the outfit he'd worn when he'd had dinner with his mom. He wished he had a suit like Joshua's or Christian's. *Someday.* He imagined himself dressed that way onstage, ready to play his trumpet.

Bex had stopped at the grocery store to pick up items on a list from Ferguson. She and her brothers had lucked out, because Ferguson and their dad were both working late then were going out to dinner after, and therefore wouldn't be home until late. Bex texted Gwilym: "I'm in the car now. I'll be home soon. Be ready to go when I get home."

"How do I look?" Clay asked. He wore a pink button-down shirt and *his* only pair of dress pants. His pants sagged around his waist.

"Where's your belt?" asked Gwilym.

"I can't wear the one I have."

"Why not?" asked Gwilym.

"The buckle is a cowboy on a horse. You wear it with jeans."

"That's the only one you own?"

"Yes. I don't need other belts. My other pants fit without a belt."

"You have to put on a belt with those pants, Clay. They're going to fall down."

"Okay," Clay said, unconvinced. "I'll put it on."

Gwilym could tell it meant a lot to Clay to look polished for their mom.

Bex stood at the bottom of the stairs. "Is Clay ready? I'll wait in the car." Gwilym observed his sister. She may not have admitted to anyone that she was excited to attend her mom's concert, but she looked especially pretty tonight. She wore a black-and-white polka dot dress and black heels. Gwilym had not seen her wear this outfit before.

Bex's long hair flowed around her face and it was accented by gold droplet earrings.

Gwilym leaned into Clay's doorway. "Are you ready?" he asked.

Clay's back was to Gwilym. His brother tapped on the keyboard of his MacBook and turned around with a big smile on his face. John Denver blared from the speakers. He sang along in his off-key alto. "Country roads . . ."

"Are you *ready*?" Gwilym asked again. Clay was set; he just needed to comb his hair.

"We gotta *go*, Clay."

Clay continued singing. "Yes, you sound just like him," Gwilym said. "Clay, stop singing and comb your hair."

His brother's smile dropped. "No one like John Denver, Gwilym." He took a comb out of his pocket and glided it through his gelled hair.

"I know, Clay, but maybe someday you could try listening to another musician."

Clay looked stunned. "John Denver's the best."

"Yeah, he's good. I guess. But there are—"

"No, Gwilym."

"I just don't understand why you insist on listening only to—" And then Gwilym closed his mouth. He looked above Clay's desk and saw the John Denver poster that had been tacked to his brother's wall as long as he could remember. "Who gave you that poster, Clay?"

"Grandma gave it to me." Clay was looking in the mirror above his dresser, smoothing his hair.

Gwilym looked closer. The corners of the poster had small tears and the sides were buckling. "Was this Mom's? Do you know? Did she like country music?"

"Grandma said it was Mom's. She had it on her wall in high school. Grandma said I could have it."

Gwilym wondered what their mom would think of Clay having her old poster on the wall of his bedroom. It had probably hung in his room since high school, or even before—perhaps since he was ten years old. *Maybe it's time he took it down.*

"I'm ready, Gwilym."

When they got into the car, Bex acted like she'd been waiting an eternity for them. Gwilym pressed his pants with his hands, and Clay patted his hair. "Are we done primping, boys? We're not going for a photo shoot. We're just going to a concert."

Right. Just going to listen to some random band. Nobody we know playing . . . certainly not the Caroline McCorkle Band . . . Gwilym let out a large breath. "Yeah, we're ready."

Gwilym knew their mom would be warming up backstage when they arrived. He wanted to go back there to see how she did it. But the thought made his whole body feel weak. He needed to sit because he was nervous and excited again. "Let's find our seats."

"Okay," said Bex, walking to their assigned seats.

As they passed the ushers, Gwilym heard one say to the other, "Yes, Caroline, the band leader. She's backstage having a breakdown. Someone heard her—"

"What is it, Gwilym?" Bex asked as she stopped at their row and stepped aside for him and Clay to go in. "You look like you're going to faint."

Before Gwilym could answer, he saw Clay pointing at Joshua, who was approaching them.

Joshua spoke in a low voice. "Would one of you or all of you mind coming with me?"

"Why?" asked Bex. She glanced at Gwilym. "Why? What's happened? Is something wrong with our mom?" Gwilym straightened, surprised at the concern in his sister's voice.

"I'm not sure," Joshua continued. "She's crying. Sobbing, really. I haven't seen your mom cry—ever."

"Yes, well. She gets it from her daughter," kidded Bex.

Bex didn't notice Joshua's interested gaze. Gwilym rolled his eyes. *Forget college-boy Buddy. Bex has a grown-up guy impressed with her.*

Joshua led them to the place at the side of the altar where the band was warming up. After tapping on the door, they heard a faint "yes" and entered the room. Their mom sat on the floor with her legs folded underneath her. Her head rested on her hands; one clutched a tissue. Her reddish-blonde curls, like Gwilym's, bounced as she coughed and sniffed. As soon as she saw her kids, she lifted her head and wiped under her eyes. "Hi," she said softly.

Even when she's been crying, her voice sounds musical. She gave one final blow into the tissue before dropping it in a wastebasket Joshua offered her. "Thanks."

She straightened her dress, which closely matched the maroon color of the sweater she'd worn at dinner. "I'm sure you weren't expecting this from me . . . but you wouldn't know what to expect from me. You don't know me, after all . . . being my fault, entirely." She sighed and pulled another tissue from the box.

Gwilym took hold of Bex's arm to keep her from saying anything, and she didn't resist. He felt that prickly sensation on his skin again.

Shifting from one foot to the other, clearly uneasy, Joshua said, "I'll be outside."

"Mom." Gwilym stepped close and squatted in front of her. "What are you doing? You have a show to do. Your band's waiting for you, and so is the audience."

She sniffed again, then turned her face up to his. Her expression was so open and vulnerable, it almost blew him back like a dandelion on a puff of air. His jaw tightened and his heart pounded.

His mom blinked. "Bex—look at you! You're beautiful. Oh, I knew you would be. And Clay. My darling Clay. What a nice-looking man you are!" From her spot on the floor she raised her hands to them. Bex gripped Clay's arm.

"Mom," Gwilym said. His voice sounded confident, not unsure like when he'd first said her name outside Tiger's Tale. "Get up."

She dropped her hands back down by her sides. "I'm sorry I left on Wednesday without seeing you. I think I honestly had a panic attack! After the concert, I suddenly became so afraid thinking about you coming back to see me. I ran. And now look at me, on the floor, a mess. I didn't plan this out very well, did I?"

"Get up, Mom," Gwilym repeated. "You've got a performance to give."

"I can't. I can't. It's everything. It's too much." She paused. Gwilym noticed her eyes change, as if she recognized something or someone. "It's like—it's everything to you—and then it's only chocolate."

"*What?*" Bex said. "Maybe we need to get a professional shrink in here."

"I've been to therapy my whole life," said Caroline. "No, you don't understand."

"*Should* we have to . . . understand?" Bex asked. "Should it be our problem?"

Gwilym sat beside his mom. "Can this wait?"

"No," she whined. "I'm sorry if I'm making everybody wait. I'm so tired."

"Aren't we all? And, right now, we're tired of you," said Gwilym. "And you're not sorry, either." He was impressed and a little surprised by his growing anger.

"Whoa," Bex whispered. His sister's approval encouraged him.

"What *about* chocolate?" asked Clay, stepping forward. He loved chocolate.

Caroline smiled. "I had a piece of chocolate someone I cared about gave me. It was my favorite kind."

"Reese's Peanut Butter Cups," said Gwilym.

She cocked her head at him. "You're right. How did you know?"

He shrugged. "You were saying? Hurry up with your story."

"Gwilym's right," agreed Bex. "You're being rude to your band and audience. And, as you know, I generally have nothing against being rude."

"Mom," pleaded Clay. "Tell us the story."

"I was given this piece of chocolate and told to eat it only on a special occasion. So I waited. And then on my birthday, he couldn't be with me."

"When Uncle Hal couldn't be with you," corrected Gwilym.

"*What? Uncle Hal?*" said Bex.

His mom chuckled. "The letters! Were they in the shed? I wondered where my letters and cards had gone! The Reese's Peanut Butter Cup wrapper must have been with them. Now, Gwilym, some were from your dad, too."

"It's true," Gwilym said, "but did Dad know you also dated Cat's uncle?"

"Okay, lots of questions for you later," Bex said.

Gwilym heard a voice from the stage. Joshua was apologizing to the audience. Something like "She'll be out in a few minutes, thank you for your patience." Anger rose from Gwilym's stomach to his throat. "Mom!"

Instead of responding to Gwilym, she focused her attention on Clay, reaching out her hands to him. He took a step closer but didn't take her hands. "I don't know if you'll understand this," she said to him.

"He's twenty, Mom," Bex informed her. "He's not stupid."

"I know, honey." She refocused on Clay. "You and your brother and sister are like that piece of chocolate I saved and wouldn't eat until exactly the right time. I waited and waited to come back to see you. I was scared about what it would be like. What would it be like to see you again after ten years? Yes, I left when you were so young and so vulnerable. But I had to see you."

"Reminds me of *The Odyssey*," mumbled Bex. "Odysseus was away from his family for twenty years. It took him ten years of trying to get home. Kind of like Mom taking ten years to return . . ." At that moment Gwilym remembered Bex had always loved reading myths and fantasy stories. Her words sparked a memory from when he was little. He had walked past her room and had seen her looking down at the fairies Grandma had woven into her rug, and she had said, "Will you fairies bring back my mom, please?"

"I've got to finish my story! I ate the chocolate I'd waited to eat, but it wasn't everything I thought it would be.

"You are as wonderful as I expected you to be. But the anticipation. The apprehension. The fear I had. Well, it wasn't as bad as I thought it might be. I hoped it all could be put back together and it would be great, like the chocolate bar. But like with a lot of life, we get attached to ideas, or how things are going to be, and then when we get them they are just more of life."

She'd built up their reunion into a whole big thing, then it turned out to be just the first step in reconnecting with them. Gwilym was surprised that he understood what his mom was trying to say.

"I don't understand," Clay said.

"It's okay," said their mom. "I'm just rambling. Sorry."

"Well, my English teacher would probably give your story a C, C+ at best," said Bex.

Gwilym opened the door to Joshua, who was waiting just outside.

"Mom, ready to go on?" He helped her stand up.

"Yes, just give me ten minutes to get my makeup fixed." She smiled at him.

Gwilym and his siblings walked out of the side of the chapel. The seats were filled again like at the last concert. He heard murmuring as he followed his siblings to their seats. Finally, the Caroline McCorkle Band came out. Their mom looked beautiful. They began the first set. Gwilym teared up. *She glows when she plays the trumpet.*

Gwilym's confrontation with his mom seemed to inspire her performance. The concert was good. *No, amazing.*

They went backstage after the concert to say goodbye. It was awkward.

"So, we leave tomorrow evening, but I'd hoped we could get together at the hotel for breakfast?" Caroline suggested. The three agreed to the plan.

Driving them home, Bex was animated. She laughed and snorted. Slapped the steering wheel and screamed with Metallica.

Clay and Gwilym remained silent until Gwilym finally decided he had to take charge. "Will you stop, Bex!"

She smiled. "Okay. I'm done." She put Metallica at a more conservative volume. "Better?" She looked in the rearview mirror at her brother.

"Better," said Clay. He stared out the window.

"Why are you so hyper, Bex?" Gwilym asked.

"I guess I like jazz better than I thought."

"And she likes Joshua," said Clay.

"I do not!" Gwilym saw that Bex couldn't keep a smile off her face. Had his sister actually noticed a guy?

Their parents were still out when the kids got home. Gwilym went to his room and put on his T-shirt and pajama bottoms. He plopped on his bed, and Baby got up next to him. He petted the dog and thought about the night. He realized he wasn't tired, so he got up and went to Bex's door. He knocked. "Can I come in?" She was propped up in bed reading *The Odyssey.* He noticed she had the turquoise mermaid drink stirrer in her hand.

He looked at the book. "I'm going to have to read that, aren't I?"

"I'm sure you will." She examined the book's cover. "It's not bad. Actually, I like it." Bex got up and returned the plastic trinket to its permanent place, the jewelry bowl on her dresser.

"You could pick English for your major, like Buddy. And you two could study together since you'll both be at FSU."

"Maybe I will."

Gwilym didn't know which part of what he'd said she was answering.

Staring at the book she said, "Odysseus was away from his family for twenty years. Ten of those were spent returning to his family."

Gwilym sat beside her.

"That's what the story's about: him telling tales, going through all this drama, searching . . ."

"What's he searching for?"

Bex opened the book flat on the bed and paged to the front. "The author of the introduction talks about the father figure, but it's more about a parent than a father. It could be a mother as easily. It's about an absent parent." Her eyes were looking at the top of her dresser.

"Yeah?" He resisted putting his arm around her shoulder. A stream of anger ran through him. He didn't like seeing his sister hurt. They rarely brought up their mom, and when the topic came up he'd prepare for her cheeks to turn red and then for her to frown.

Bex read to him, "'If the parent is not there, then the child may ask: Where do I get those feelings of protection, authority, confidence, know-how, and wisdom?' You see, Gwilym, Mom left without laying this foundation for us, even for me and Clay, who were older. And we all love Ferguson, but she's not our mom. And she wasn't responsible for our development." Bex returned to the page: "'How does the child get these things it needs in order to live its life if the father figure is

absent or unavailable or unable to provide them?'"
She closed the book and looked at Gwilym.

His eyes widened. "Am I supposed to understand? Because I don't think I understand."

"No, not yet." She stood and slid the book into her school bag.

Gwilym got up too, then said impishly, "Maybe you should ask Buddy about it."

"Will you stop!" said Bex, smiling. "Go away."

JUNE

Gwilym and Bex were at the side of the house giving Baby and Bear baths. He was hosing Baby off, while Bex crouched, ready to catch the dog with a big bath towel.

"Come here Baby, come here, boy." She grabbed him and kissed his nose as she rubbed his head. "Good boy!"

Gwilym began soaping Bear when Clay walked out the laundry room door. "Mom called me," he announced, as proud as if he'd presented himself with a ribbon for a scavenger hunt picture.

"What'd she say?" Bex asked. Sensing Bex's grip on him loosening, Baby bolted and immediately rolled in the grass. "Baby, you bad boy."

"You are supposed to put him on the leash before you let him go," Clay informed her.

"Thanks," said Bex. "I'll remember that next time. After I've bathed these beasts for the millionth time."

"Clay, what did Mom say?" Gwilym asked.

"She will be at the lake in about an hour," answered Clay.

"Does she know where to meet us?" Gwilym asked.

"I would hope she remembers that we fished on Aunt River's dock," said Bex.

"She remembered," Clay reassured his sister. Then changing the subject, Clay said, "Gwilym, you can ride your new bike for the first time."

"I *can* ride my new bike! You're right, Clay!" Gwilym had finally made enough money from his deliveries to buy a new bike.

❧

Gwilym stood at the back of his bike, where he'd attached a wicker basket that contained a beach towel. He had wrapped Grandpa's tackle box inside the towel. His sister, brother, and mom had already made the trek down the dirt hill and were on the dock. Gwilym kept his gaze on the lake. He'd forgotten the colors of the water of Lake Saturday. White crests of the waves pushed toward the shore, held up by a combination of maroon-brown and blue-green. The motion of the water soothed his mind.

The wood dock with rusty nails bounced as he stepped onto it. When he caught up to his family he noticed a peaceful quiet among them. Each was focusing on their line. He selected a green fluorescent plastic worm from the tackle box and attached it to the hook. Then he dropped his line in the water, into the streaks of sunlight bouncing off the surface. The small fish—he thought they were called guppies—moved with the current. He listened to the waves crashing against the shore and a motorboat in the distance. A sunfish wandered around his lure. He thought of the fish as kids, each daring the other to go for the bait. Which one would be bold enough; which one would give into the peer pressure? None of the fish had decided to yet.

"I got one!" Clay yelled. He pulled it out of the water, made a quick motion with his fingers that released the hook from its mouth, then he dropped the fish back into the water.

"Nice job," said Bex, moving closer to Clay. She looked relaxed, with her head tilted to one side.

Their mom grinned as she said, "Bex, do you remember fishing when you were little?"

Gwilym didn't have any memories of fishing here with his siblings and mom. His chest swelled with envy.

"Yes," Bex answered. "I remember fishing here. I remember Grandpa here, too."

"He would always join us fishing," their mom said.

"Got another one!" Clay flung the fish onto the dock.

"Geez," said Bex, laughing. "It's not a competition."

"Oh," yelped Caroline, "I've caught one. First one of the day for me." She seemed to have been tuning out her children's conversation. She kept the small fish on her line a moment before pulling it out of the water and quickly unhooking it. "I miss this. I haven't done this in so long," she said as she released the fish. "I'd like to do this with you guys whenever I'm in town—if that sounds good. I thought maybe it could be our new tradition."

"Yeah!" Clay grinned from ear to ear.

"Sounds good," agreed Bex. "As long as you don't suggest fishing in the winter."

Gwilym didn't answer, but his chest loosened. He liked that they were beginning a new tradition. And this time, he was a part of it.

"I only fished in winter once," their mom said, "with your grandpa when I was a kid. It wasn't fun."

"Dad and Grandpa took me fishing in the winter on the frozen lake one time," Clay told them. "I liked it." He paused. "I wish Grandpa was still with us." The others nodded.

"So, Clay, what's the next art exhibition you're helping install at the library gallery?" asked Gwilym.

"It is prints of pictures of cutouts that an artist named Henri Matisse made. They are from a collection called *Jazz*. One of the pictures is on the cover of a Wynton Marsalis album."

"You're joking," said Gwilym. "Are you sure?"

"Sure of what?" Clay jerked up his line. The fish on it escaped. "Shoot."

"Clay," Gwilym asked. "Are you sure the Matisse collection is called *Jazz*?"

"Why do you think I wouldn't know what the name of it is? I know what the name of the exhibit is, Gwilym."

"Why are you questioning him?" Bex scolded.

"Because that's the artwork Benton showed Cat and me. We looked at two pictures and I tried to make music with my trumpet to go with them."

"Really?" said Caroline. "I haven't seen these works. Wynton Marsalis is the leader of the Jazz at Lincoln Center Orchestra. He and his colleagues took famous works of art and created jazz pieces to go with them. I think the album's called *Jazz and Art*. Music and paintings share so many similarities—textures, colors, layers, line, form."

"That's what Benton was showing us."

"Tell Mom the other thing that's related to music, Clay," said Bex. "What are you listening to now? And who got you into it?"

Clay's round cheeks grew red. "I'm listening to zydeco."

"You are?" Their mom grinned. "Have you retired your John Denver records?"

"No. I still listen to them, but I like listening to other types of music now."

Bex interjected, "And why did you start listening to zydeco, Clay?"

With his cheeks glowing, he stared at the water. "Grace played it for me."

"Who's Grace?" their mom asked, smiling at him.

"Grace is my classmate. She's very pretty," he said, looking at his mom now. "She's from Louisiana. Zydeco is also called Creole Cajun music."

"Clay, tell Mom who's on your wall now instead of the John Denver poster," Gwilym said, steering away from the subject of Grace for his brother.

Clay relaxed his shoulders and lifted his chin. "I have a poster of Buckwheat Zydeco on my wall now." Their mom nodded in approval.

"Speaking of different types of music," Bex said. "What's the progress with the Metallica and Caroline McCorkle collaboration?" During the most recent meal the four of them had shared, Bex had come up with the idea of their mom's band collaborating with her favorite band.

"Yes, I was going to update you on that. We're planning to do it. We're working on dates when we'll all be available." Bex's eyes widened. Their mom continued, "This all just happened in the last couple of days, things coming together. So I wasn't keeping any news from you. I just found out. I'll let you know as soon as I get more news. I promise."

"Okay," said Bex. "Do you think I could meet them?"

"Possibly." Her mom winked at her.

"Bex's biggest dream come true," said Gwilym. "Her life would then be complete."

"Maybe she'll faint in front of them! That would be funny. My cool sister, Bex, fainting in front of her favorite band, Metallica." Clay giggled.

"That's not nice, Clay," said Bex, laughing too. "Maybe after that, Mom could make an album with Buckwheat Zydeco. Then I can laugh at you fainting."

"Now there's another great idea," said their mom.

Filled with good spirit, they went back to concentrating on fishing.

"Next time you're here with the band, could I watch you guys practice?" Gwilym asked.

"I'm sure the guys would enjoy that—and I certainly would! They're very much into sharing tips with young jazz musicians, wherever they are in their music level. Then someday you can play a gig with us."

"Playing with you and your band would be amazing!" Gwilym's stomach flip-flopped with excitement at the thought of what he could learn from sitting in on just one of their sessions, let alone playing with them!

Bex and Clay had moved away from him and his mom to the end of the dock. He wanted to ask her something privately, and now was a good time.

"Mom?"

"Yes?"

"I have a question—"

"I'll try to answer it. Oh!" She pulled up her line just as a fish slipped off the lure. "Darn."

She seemed distracted by her fishing efforts, but Gwilym didn't want to miss this chance to talk to her alone, even though his heart pounded. "So when I was arranging my music studio in the shed, I found these letters, as you figured out. They were addressed to you."

"Yes. I had forgotten about them. What do you want to know about them?"

"Do you want them back?" he said quickly. It hadn't occurred to him until now that she might want them back.

"No." She smiled but didn't look at him. "Keep them if you'd like." Then she looked at him inquisitively.

"I figured out some were from Cat's Uncle Hal and some were from Dad. I wanted to know why they were in the shed."

"Your dad and I dated. Then we broke up, and Uncle Hal and I dated for a little while. But then your dad and I got back together. Hal was fun to hang around with. We both liked listening to jazz. Your dad just couldn't get why we loved it so much." She laughed, then paused. "I didn't care that your dad didn't understand jazz. I loved him. He could have listened to any kind of music and it wouldn't have mattered to me. I think that's how you know you love someone. Their tastes may be the opposite of yours—they may be hideous!—but you don't care. You don't care because you love them. You love them so much you'll listen to John Denver even though it makes your ears feel like they'll implode. You'll even hang a John Denver poster in your bedroom."

Gwilym laughed. He was comfortable being with her. It almost seemed like she'd been in his life all along. He was relieved to know his mom had loved his dad.

"What are you guys talking about?" asked Bex, walking down the dock toward them. "Clay's killing it at this fish-catching thing. I say we make him stop and eat lunch."

"Sounds good," agreed their mom.

They spread out the feast on a nearby picnic table, ate their sandwiches and chips, then Bex's chocolate cookies, which were the best.

Gwilym lifted his face to the sun. Birds flew by and a branch swayed with the weight of two squirrels leaping onto it. Suddenly a question popped into his head. "Mom, did you pick Coltrane for my middle name? Did Dad like it too or want something else? Nobody's told me why—"

"Gwilym," Bex kiddingly scolded him. "Shut up. We don't need everything answered today. Sit and enjoy. We'll see Mom again." Bex glanced at their mom, who nodded.

He closed his eyes and concentrated until in his head he could hear the first couple of notes of Coltrane's "Giant Steps."

The four went back to their fishing. No one spoke for a long time. A calmness settled over them. At one point Gwilym looked over at his sister and was surprised to see her frowning. His chest tightened. She was going to say something to ruin this moment.

"I haven't gotten over you leaving, Mom." Bex was staring at the water.

Their mom's shoulders dropped. She didn't say anything at first, then she said, "Has there been anything that's helped you to cope, anybody who was—"

Bex interrupted. "I tell myself that if I can make it to the end of the day, then I will be okay. I have survived another day. I have made it through the pain once more."

Gwilym didn't know that this was how his sister had coped all these years. He'd grown up with conflicting feelings. He'd felt guilty because his siblings had spent more time with his mom than he had, so they'd suffered more by her leaving; at the same time, he felt jealous *because* they had had more time with her. And then sometimes he felt it was his fault that she left them.

Clay's voice broke into Gwilym's thoughts. "I just missed you," he said.

Their mom smiled sadly at Clay. "Only three things have helped me with the grief I've lived with since I left you three and your dad: having a routine, being in nature, and seeing details of beauty around me."

"Explain," said Bex. She set her fishing pole down and crossed her arms.

"I have a morning routine and an evening routine. In between, I have my music. I try to walk every day in nature, if I can. Or if we're on tour in a city, then I walk the streets. I like walking at night in the city, which drives Joshua and Christian crazy. They become my big brothers, worried something's going to happen to me." She laughed softly. "But being in nature helps me most with the heartache."

Gwilym looked at her. He hadn't realized she might feel the same ache he did. "And then I concentrate on details in my life, like playing every note perfectly, and looking at simple details around me that make me happy. Like, say, a button."

"A button?" Bex laughed. "That's funny. I hadn't thought of a button as being beautiful." She tugged her ponytail. "So, you've been hurting too. Well, I guess that makes me feel a little better."

"Bex," Clay quietly pleaded.

"What?"

"Don't be mean," he replied.

"Don't be mean . . ." She let go of her hair.

"I'd hoped we could start a new tradition here, fishing together," Caroline said to them. "I know the lost years can't ever be replaced. We probably won't ever lose the ache, but I believe this can help."

"I think it can, Mom," said Gwilym. He tapped his fishing pole on the dock, then looked up. "Bex, what are you doing?"

His sister was standing in front of a group of birch trees. "Do you hear that? It sounds like meowing." Bex leaned down in the tall grass between the trees and pulled up a gray kitten. It meowed softly as she held it. The others put down their fishing poles and joined her.

"It's so cute," said Clay, petting its tiny head.

Their mom stroked its back. "You're so sweet, aren't you! Do you remember Baby and Bear were this little when we got them?" Clay nodded. Bex smiled.

"I'm keeping it," Bex said. She rubbed its face on her cheek. "I'm calling you Oddie, after Odysseus, so it'll fit if you're a girl or a boy." She handed it to Clay.

"He looks like a boy," said Clay, carefully turning it around.

As he held the kitten, the others gathered the equipment and headed for their bikes. Clay said he could hold the tackle box while riding his bike. Bex was in charge of the fishing rods. Gwilym carefully wrapped Oddie in the beach towel and secured the towel in the basket. For a moment, their mom stood beside her rental car and Gwilym, Clay, and Bex by their bikes. Gwilym was the first to step forward and give her a hug. She hesitated before folding her arms around him. Then Clay hugged her tightly, which made his mom laugh. Bex stepped forward. Gwilym wondered who would initiate a hug. Caroline stretched out her arms and Bex slid into them. He smiled.

"I will see you three soon. I promise."

His stomach flip-flopped with excitement. Was she telling the truth? Her big smile told him she meant it.

He and his siblings waved to their mom as she drove away.

Then Gwilym smiled at the fluffy gray head peeking out of the basket. *Oddie, you'll always remind me of this day with my mom.*

ACKNOWLEDGMENTS

I am forever grateful for my family and friends, for their support and enthusiasm for my work (see the list of these special people in *Drawing with Whitman*). I thank my readers: Brennen Hocenic, Natalie Anne Stocky, Kathryn Fox, Ruby Suereth, Sophie Suereth, and Adelaide Pannell. I appreciate Kat Idelman's guidance in trumpet playing. Once again, Gina Hogan Edwards, my friend and editor, is an immeasurable mentor to me. My writing life has been so enriched by being a part of Gina's writing group, Women Writing for Change (love you ladies!). A thank you goes to my friend Mary Veal for passing on her knowledge of Metallica. I am so happy that Christina Henry de Tessan and Ingrid Emerick had the faith in me and my books to invite me to become a part of Girl Friday Books.

From Girl Friday Productions, I want to thank my project manager Alexander Rigby, production editor Laura Dailey, art director Paul Barrett, editors Sharon Turner Mulvihill and Melody Moss, and everyone else whom I haven't named here. And a big *Hooray!* to the very important artists who contributed their amazing artwork to the Sourland Mountain series: Kristina Swarner, illustrator of the book covers for *Listen* and *Drawing with Whitman*, and Kristin Heron, who illustrated the Sourland Mountain map.

GLOSSARY OF JAZZ MUSICIANS

Just a small selection of jazz musicians to get to know

Louis Armstrong (1901–1971): trumpeter and singer. The "King of Jazz" made trumpet sounds with his voice, called scatting. He was the first jazz musician to write an autobiography, titled *Swing That Music.*

Count Basie (1904–1984): bandleader, pianist, and songwriter. His famous swing band, the Count Basie Orchestra, got its start playing in Kansas City nightclubs. The "Count" said, "If you play a tune and a person don't tap their feet, don't play the tune." *(Quotation from* J Is for Jazz *by Ann Ingalls, illustrated by Maria Corte Maidagan.)*

George Benson (born 1943): guitarist and singer. He successfully combined jazz, pop, and R & B into a style of music called smooth jazz. When he was seven he played the ukulele in a drugstore for a few dollars.

Cab Calloway (1907–1994): bandleader, singer, dancer, and actor. He was a regular performer at the Cotton Club in New York City during the swing era. For contemporary movie audiences, he is best known for his performance of "Minnie the Moocher" in *The Blues Brothers.*

John Coltrane (1926–1967): saxophonist. Considered a musical giant, the brooding sound of his saxophone is still one of the most recognizable in jazz. He was influenced by elements of traditional African and Indian music. Playing jazz was a deeply spiritual experience for him.

Miles Davis (1926–1991): trumpeter. He received a trumpet on his thirteenth birthday, and began working on his own sound. He played what is called cool jazz and a number of other styles of jazz.

Duke Ellington (1899–1974): bandleader, pianist, and composer. An originator of big-band jazz, he played more than twenty thousand performances. He studied painting before becoming a jazz musician.

Ella Fitzgerald (1917–1996): singer. She was nicknamed the "First Lady of Jazz" for her quality of phrasing, timing, and a "hornlike" improvisational style, particularly her scat singing.

Nnenna Freelon (born 1954): singer, composer, and playwright. She is a Grammy-nominated jazz vocalist. She learned to appreciate all types of music by singing in church and listening to her father's Count Basie recordings.

Dizzy Gillespie (1917–1993): trumpeter, singer, bandleader, composer, and educator. He was a trumpet virtuoso and improviser. He combined layers of harmony and rhythm never before heard in jazz music.

Benny Goodman (1909–1986): clarinetist and bandleader. Called the "King of Swing," he was ten years old when he learned to play the clarinet. Along with being a famous swing bandleader, he was also well known for rejecting segregation by including Black musicians in the Benny Goodman Band.

Roy Hargrove (1969–2018): trumpeter. A two-time Grammy Award winner, he was an important jazz musician of his generation, bringing together the bebop tradition and hip-hop and R & B. He created a nonprofit performance place called The Jazz Gallery.

Billie Holiday (1915–1959): singer. Her career spanned almost thirty years and influenced jazz and pop music. She was known for her very expressive and emotional vocals.

Wynton Marsalis (born 1961): trumpeter, composer, educator, and director of Jazz at Lincoln Center. He is a strong advocate for and promoter of classical and jazz music, especially to young audiences. He is a part of a large family of famous jazz musicians.

Christian McBride (born 1972): bassist, composer, arranger, and educator. He has played on more than three hundred recordings and is a six-time Grammy Award winner. He is a champion of the past, present, and future of jazz music.

Susannah McCorkle (1946–2001): singer. She brought an emotional intensity to the words she sang, much like Billie Holiday, and she could make a rhythm sound like a conversation. She was also a published author who won awards for her short fiction.

Thelonious Monk (1917–1982): pianist and improviser. He wore funny hats during his performances. He played music that would unexpectedly start and stop and had sharp, angular melodies.

Charlie Parker (1920–1955): saxophonist. He created a new music style called bebop. Known as "the Bird," his phrasing, innovation, and the speed at which he played the sax made him a legend in the jazz world.

Joshua Redman (born 1969): saxophonist and composer. His father, Dewey Redman, was a famous saxophonist like his son. Some of his early influences were John Coltrane, Aretha Franklin, the Beatles, the Police, and Led Zeppelin.

Mary Lou Williams (1910–1981): pianist, arranger, composer, and educator. She wrote hundreds of compositions and arrangements, and recorded more than one hundred records. She was a mentor to Thelonious Monk, Charlie Parker, Miles Davis, and Dizzy Gillespie.

Cassandra Wilson (born 1955): singer, songwriter, and producer. She incorporates blues, country, and folk music into her work. She is a Grammy Award winner and received an Honorary Doctorate in Music from Berklee College of Music.

RESOURCES

Books

The Art of Jazz: A Visual History by Alyn Shipton (One interesting quotation from this observes, "Socially acceptable roles for women in jazz have been primarily restricted to vocalists, sometimes pianists . . . yet women musicians have played every instrument in every style and era of jazz history.")

Birth of the Cool: How Jazz Great Miles Davis Found His Sound by Kathleen Cornell Berman, illustrated by Keith Henry Brown

Duke Ellington written and illustrated by Mike Venezia

Duke Ellington: His Life in Jazz by Stephanie Stein Crease (Includes fun music activities)

J Is for Jazz by Ann Ingalls, illustrated by Maria Corte Maidagan

Jam!: The Story of Jazz Music by Jeanne Lee
Jazz by Henri Matisse
Jazz by Walter Dean Myers, illustrated by Christopher Myers
Josephine: The Dazzling Life of Josephine Baker by Patricia Hruby Powell, illustrated by Christian Robinson
Louis Armstrong: King of Jazz by Patricia and Fredrick McKissack
Muddy: The Story of Blues Legend Muddy Waters by Michael Mahin, illustrated by Evan Turk
The Odyssey, by Homer. Translated by Robert Fagles. 1997 Penguin Classics Deluxe Edition
Seeing Jazz: Artists and Writers on Jazz edited by Elizabeth Goldson
Who was Louis Armstrong? by Yona McDonough, illustrated by John O'Brien

Websites

America's Story, from America's Library: www.americaslibrary.gov
Jazz at Lincoln Center: https://jazzatlincolncenter.squarespace.com

Jazz for Young People Curriculum: https://academy.jazz.org/jfyp/jfyp-curriculum
Jazz History Online: https://jazzhistoryonline.com
Traditional Jazz Curriculum Kit: https://jazzednet.org/tradjazzproject
Jazz, a film by Ken Burns: www.pbs.org/show/jazz

ABOUT THE AUTHOR

Before becoming an award-winning author, Kristin McGlothlin was the assistant curator of education at the Norton Museum of Art, where she designed and managed the Norton's art and music programs. She has a BA in art history and a BA and MA in English. Her master's thesis was on the author and illustrator Edward Gorey.

McGlothlin wrote and created the artwork for the children's picture book *Andy's Snowball Story*, about the contemporary artist Andy Goldsworthy. Her poem "California T-Shirt" was published in the literary magazine *Coastlines*, and "Roman Ruins in a Modern City" won a haiku contest and was read on *Travel with Rick Steves*. McGlothlin's short story "The Red Door" was one of twenty-three finalists among more than four hundred entries in the 2018 Florida Weekly Writing Challenge.

Drawing with Whitman was her debut middle-grade novel. It was the winner of the 2019 Moonbeam Silver Medal for Pre-Teen Fiction and received an honorable mention in the 2020 Readers' Favorite International Book Awards for children grades four through six. *Drawing with Whitman* is the first book in the four-book Sourland Mountain series, and *Listen* is the second. A writer since she was thirteen, now, like a million years later, she has settled upon writing as her career. She lives in Jupiter, Florida.

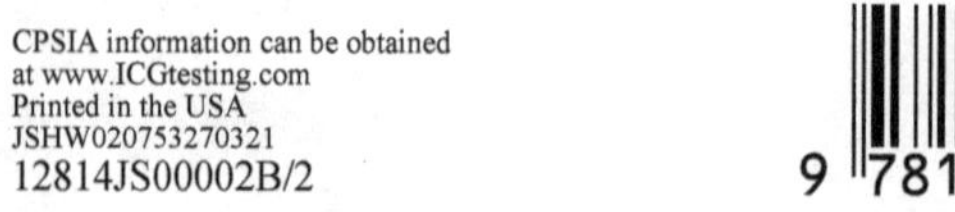

CPSIA information can be obtained
at www.ICGtesting.com
Printed in the USA
JSHW020753270321
12814JS00002B/2

9 781736 357910